A SHOT OF
BRANDI

David S. Tanz

iUniverse, Inc.
Bloomington

A Shot of Brandi

Copyright © 2012 David S. Tanz

iUniverse books may be ordered through booksellers or by contacting:

iUniverse
1663 Liberty Drive
Bloomington, IN 47403
www.iuniverse.com
1-800-Authors (1-800-288-4677)

ISBN: 978-1-4620-6681-0 (sc)
ISBN: 978-1-4620-6682-7 (hc)
ISBN: 978-1-4620-6683-4 (e)

Library of Congress Control Number: 2011960251

Printed in the United States of America

iUniverse rev. date: 4/10/2012

Prologue

Rick Grosse was as stoked as a Christmas Yule-log fire. It was opening day at Citizens Bank Park, home of the Philadelphia Phillies. Every year, Doug Brady, self-proclaimed pretzel king of Philadelphia, would bring a group of his fifty closest high school friends to the home opener. His first-base box came complete with cheese steaks, assorted hoagies, an endless stream of alcohol, and, of course, his famous pretzels. Billboards covered all major thoroughfares between the Philadelphia areas straight down to Atlantic City. His product was actually tasty, which made his franchise a hot new business venture from New England to the left coast.

Rick Grosse was one of the lucky fifty invited. He took the twenty-minute drive down Broad Street, arriving at the surrounding parking lots that serviced the several arenas that housed the professional sports teams representing the city. He was looking forward to seeing some old faces but more so to the game. He was a diehard fan. He already knew the face who would not be there.

He entered the stadium with his VIP pass and took the elevator to the private boxes. Once his ticket was rechecked, he entered the crowded lounge. In the back of his mind he was hoping Brandi McCugh might be in attendance. She had been his teen love, "the one who got away." They had been a fixture as a couple during his late teens, but he had messed it up like most teen lovers. His hopes to see her again were eternal, even if a little whimsical.

He circled the large box and took the two steps up to the bar area in order to improve his view of the gathering. Several women were in attendance, but, as expected, Brandi wasn't. He assumed she hadn't changed much in the three decades since he had last seen her. As he turned to get a beer, someone tapped his shoulder.

"Ricky! Ricky Grosse, my man, great to see you."

He recognized the voice of Bobby Conigliaro, his friend since first grade.

"Yo, Bobby C. Yo dog. You look marvelous," he said in his best Billy Crystal impersonation, made famous in the old *Saturday Night Live* routines.

"Lookin' for your girl Friday?" Bobby asked with a laugh.

"Yeah, yeah, somethin' like that," Rick confessed.

He and Bobby had gotten suspended in high school. They'd been caught drinking on a field trip to Longwood Gardens, an arboretum in Chester County twenty miles south west of the city. Rick was a rebel then. His parents put few restrictions on him, giving him the freedom to learn by his mistakes. They had never pressured him to go to college or have a direction in life, as many parents of the late-seventies had. This was apparent in his current lifestyle, and at times he wished they had pushed him toward some success … legal success.

The two reminisced, drank, and laughed. Almost at the same time they had mentioned they had both dropped the *y* from their youthful names, the added letter making them sound like children. Bobby, now Bob, showed pictures of his son's graduation, mentioning that he was starting his freshman year at Penn State and was damn proud of him. Bob mentioned he wanted to mingle, and he left with the both of them glad they had talked.

Before he could turn around to refresh his beer, Rick was approached by his host, Doug Brady, and received a vice-like handshake. Doug mentioned he was happy Rick came and flashed a wink. Several years ago, Rick had set Doug and his investment bankers up with a night on the town. In the fashion of *"Full Service Concierges,"* he orchestrated dinner at Morimoto. The extra icing was the geisha-clad hookers who served them in a private dining area downstairs. The result was a large loan for Doug's company, which now resulted in hundreds of franchises.

Doug's wife, Emily, entered the conversation, which dramatically changed the topic. They too exchanged pleasantries and gave a brief recent history of her daughters' successes. One was just married, the other going to medical school, and the third taking an active part in learning the family business.

After the pair left to greet the others, Rick started thinking. He had never married. He was childless (he assumed), never learning the outcome of Brandi's pregnancy. He also realized he had no true profession. Not that these thoughts were like a lightbulb going off in his head, but they had been intensified by seeing the success and families of others.

Rick's mind also drifted to another of his many contacts: Julian Gando, an associate of Grosse's who spent most of his personal time running between New York and Philadelphia. Over a shared lunch of filet mignon and crab cakes the idea of the class reunion had been brought up. Gando happened to mention past loves, stirring up old feelings of longing. Rick had to smile and agree.

"Hell yeah, the reunion's stirrin' things up," Rick had told him. *"If there's a chance of seeing Brandi McCough, I'll eat a vending cart full of pretzels to do it!"*

As the game began, many took the cushioned chairs with the unobstructed view of the field, while others stood and watched on the several plasma television sets that hung every several feet. Rick talked with friends and acquaintances, reliving old times and filling each other in on their current statuses. As far as Rick was concerned, the highlight of the day was not the reunion but the seven-run second inning the home team had produced. The guests were loud and boisterous, cheering louder as more runs were scored and more alcohol was consumed. The game ended with an 11–2 routing of the Florida Marlins. Tomorrow's sports pages would sing the team's praises and no doubt mention that they were that much closer to clinching a spot in the playoffs. A little early for those predictions, but the city's working-class fans loved a winner.

As the game ended and the crowd dispersed, Rick recalled one his father's favorite sayings and words of advice: *"If they write about you in the newspaper, it's always better to be on the back page than the front."* Rick laughed and thought that it was better not to be in the newspaper at all, especially a man in his profession.

He flagged down the bartender to order his favorite drink. "Shot of brandy!" he called, smiling to himself. From across the room, Bobby C. smiled at him and gave a thumbs-up.

PART ONE

CHAPTER 1

Ricky Grosse grew up on Moyamensing Avenue in Philadelphia. He would refer to it as the gateway between South Philly and Center City. The neighborhood was filled with Asian markets, Wawa convenience stores, and the corner bodega that would sell cigarettes to minors and let you hang out, too. Wawa is the Delaware Valley's answer to 7-11 or Cumberland Farms. It is like comparing a Lexus to a Hyundai. The stores are clean, known for varied gourmet coffees and have every convenience one may need. It is open 24/7, 365 days a year and the staff is courteous and polite. Hot dogs don't look like they have been rotating for several weeks and they have the complete lines of another Philly delicacy, Tastykake. What more could you ask for at three in the morning coming off a night of partying? On any given day one could hear hip hop, salsa, or classic rock intermingling down various blocks. Except for the character, street names, and history it was not so different from its closest big-city neighbors of New York and Baltimore.

The architecture displayed a mix of Philly-style row homes and decaying, stucco-covered walls badly in need of repair. There were churches protruding with ornate Doric accents as well as the gated stone structures built to endure the ages. Recreation areas were not lost as one could pass concrete baseball diamonds painted with day-glow orange bases or pothole-ridden basketball courts with net-less rims.

Ricky's father had worked for SEPTA, the city's regional transportation line driving the elevated trains down Frankford Avenue or on an occasional maintenance vehicle when the snows took their toll on Philadelphia commuters. He was a hardworking, hard playing

3

man who was greatly admired by his son. All he asked of Ricky was to keep his nose clean and stay out of the realm of trouble for teenage kids growing up in the seventies. His mother worked four afternoons a week at St Paul's, cooking for the priests and was paid under the table. She would always say that you couldn't hide it from the big guy upstairs and taxes would be collected one way or another. The income helped support her husband, Ricky, and Rick's sister, Jolene, who was four years younger.

In high school, Rick managed to stay out of major trouble but still liked to play a bit on the edge. Senior year he was taking bets on football, using those strip sheets that commanded odds 1–1.5 points higher than Vegas and with parlays whose prizes were about the same as getting a diamond ring in a Crackerjack box. Business boomed and he teamed up with a jock named Carlson Mickels, who liked a good running mate. Carlson added constituents to Rick's sideline bookmaking.

Now about thirty years later, Ricky, dropping the youthful *y,* and Carl, dropping the *son,* were still at it. They had set up a sweet business near Locust Street called *Full Service Concierges.* The business plan was simple. Throughout their lives they both had bounced in and out of trouble and jail but without any major felonies. Rick had served a small stint in Allenwood for numbers, breaking and entering, and false identification, all pleaded down to misdemeanors with little incarceration time. Rick could be considered an anomaly of sorts, being able to mix it up with Philly street lingo or sport a $2000 Ralph Lauren suit with his upscale clientele.

Carl styled himself after all-American mobster Henry Hill, hanging with some "made" Mafia guys and doing some numbers collecting, loan sharking, and basically whatever was asked of him short of crimes of a violent nature. Their paths crossed over two decades, and they decided to start *Full Service,* which would offer a kaleidoscope of hard-to-get venues in the City of Brotherly Love.

The company would supply things of *need* to a growing network, spread by word of mouth, to those who wanted something and wanted it yesterday. If one was coming to Philly and needed a tough reservation at a restaurant, he would call *Full Service.* If he wanted Phillies playoff tickets, call them up. They could supply a date for the night too. Simply choose the age, skin tone, length, and girth, and they would produce.

If anyone wanted to place five dimes on the Eagles, call. If he needed an eight-ball of cocaine, an unregistered gun, or even if they needed a broken taillight, they would oblige. As with all pleasures and needs in life, they came with a price, but they would always please.

Rick and Carl had connections with the South Philly Mafia, some Rastafarians, and even some Russians on the fringe living in northeast Philly (a moderate income area on the fringes of Bucks County). The area was filled with Russian signs, which confused even those living in the area. There were ground rules, and assaults, murders, and any job that could possibly result in years in the slammer were farmed out to these groups. Rick and Carl could put anyone in touch with a little rougher crowd, but it was not for them. They catered to Hollywood types, DC politicos, and Fortune 500 executives. But anyone in the low-six-figure bracket and referred to as "gold" could pick his poison.

Business was good. No, it was great. Even in this so-called slumping economy, there were still the haves and have-nots. Philadelphia had developed an east-coast charm, partially due to its rich history. Great restaurants, popular sports teams, and after-hour nightlife added to the menu of services that *Full Service Concierges* could offer.

Rick sat behind the wheel of his classic RX-7 as he headed up I-76. He had some business to take care of. *Nothing personal, all business,* he reminded himself. It wasn't a pleasant task but something he had to do. *Sink or swim. It's him or me.* All types of rationalizations breached his thoughts. Unpleasant in one respect but necessary in the other.

He took the exit at the Philadelphia Zoo and waded through the traffic. The radio was set to classic rock as the Stones chorused, *"And I won't forget to put roses on your grave."* The warm summer day brought out multitudes of families, day camp busses, and the slew of tourists that filtered into the City of Brotherly Love. But there was little love in Rick's thoughts, only disdain for his partner. And of course revenge.

He turned down a side street and approached a cordoned off construction project with a closed gate and a man in a blue hardhat sitting by the entrance. The guard watched him approach and rolled back the security gate in order to let the car pass into the construction zone. A big sign read in large black capital letters:

KEEP OUT
DEMOLITION SITE

Rick rolled down the window and bellowed, "Joe-wee, yo."

"Yo, Rick, wasn't sure yous was comin."

"Ya know, I have some business to attend to," he responded.

"Yo, no way, I don't want to know what kinda business or nuttin' like that," Joe said.

Rick stuck his balled-up fist, which contained two hundred-dollar bills out the window and unfolded his hand over Joey's open palm. The bills fell neatly into his grasp, and a smile appeared on his face.

"Thanks, dude, class, nuttin' but class," Joey added as he slipped the bills into his open shirt pocket. "Ya got about thirty-five minutes before ya gotta haul your ass outta here."

Rick nodded. "Thanks, bro." He winked, shifted into first gear, and headed up the steep ramp of the dilapidated parking garage.

CHAPTER II

The RX-7 climbed the steep incline of the old garage as it banked around in one big right-hand spiral. He imagined it must feel like what those NASCAR drivers do for hours on end. Just around and around. *Can you really call racing a sports event with thousands of screaming idiots cheering them on, waiting for the sound of metal on metal?* He shook his head at the errant thought.

The sign read **Level 4** and Rick turned the car to the middle of the parking area. Pieces of cement littered the floor, and the dust covered the archaic walls that were not open to the view of the Frankford El. He nestled the car up to one of the supporting stone pillars and got out.

"I hope you were not too uncomfortable over the past several hours, my dear Carl. Cuffs not too tight?"

His partner had his arms stretched out over his head as he lay on the ground. Around his wrists was a thick rope wrapped around the pole, and his ankles were laced with plastic zip ties.

"What the hell am I doing here? What are you thinking!" Carl exclaimed.

"There, there now. A little politeness might be in order. I could have hog tied you face-down with your pretty little head lying in rat crap," Rick chided.

"You're not the most subtle guy around, so tell me what the fuck I'm doing—no, what the fuck are *we* doing here?"

"Glad you asked!" Rick replied. He removed a bright electrical display clock and placed it on the roof of his car with a slam that made Carl jump. It read 24:36.

"Do you know what this signifies, Carl?" he said in a whimsical tone. "Wanna venture a guess?"

"Not in the least," Carl replied in a flat tone with a taste of anxiety. His hands were shaking, and he did what he could to keep the rattling of his cuffs to a minimum.

"It's a timer. It happens to be your doomsday clock because when it expires, so do you. What I would like to do next is explain to you why you are here and what has gotten you in this precarious situation."

Beads of sweat were beginning to form on Carl's forehead as the early morning humidity filled the stale air. Sunlight bled into the parking garage from the open portals as the day rippled the atmosphere into visible waves of heat.

"This is fucking ridiculous, so just untie me and we can talk this out," Carl shouted. He was sweating even as the heat was just beginning to climb. Beads of perspiration ran down his face and stung the corners of his eyes.

Rick pulled out a Glock 38, a lightweight .38 caliber weapon with a ten-round magazine. Quick, easy, precise. He pointed at the ceiling, firing two quick rounds into the cement above their heads. "Shut the hell up and listen," Rick yelled.

Carl swallowed deeply, avoiding the menacing gaze of Rick's beady eyes. He had seen him blow up like this, and interrupting his ranting was not a good option. Even as the concrete chips dropped into his face and hair he did what he could to remain in control of his emotions.

"Go on," Carl murmured.

"Now that I have your undivided attention, I will." Rick pulled a small syringe out of his top pocket and tapped its side. "Rocuronium bromide. Familiar with this, Carl? It's used in the operating room before they put you out for surgery. It's a muscle relaxant. A small dose will basically render you motionless. You won't be able to do a thing. But your mind will be alive. You will hear everything I say but will be unable to respond because you have no control over your lips. Pretty sweet, huh, Carl? A lunch gift from our good friend Gando."

Rick strode over to Carl and plunged the syringe in, the chorus of protesting screams unaffecting him. He turned and glanced at the clock, which now read 21:00. He still had plenty of time and would use every last minute to drill his point right down Carl's throat.

He waited as Carl's mouth went numb and slack, his eyes grew still, and his blinking ceased.

He started his soliloquy. "Several weeks ago I spoke to our boy Chuck down at the Trump. We exchanged pleasantries, and he casually mentioned that Paul Ascott had been down there. And not only that, he had the twins with him. Didn't we usually arrange those meetings for a fee? Then I ran into Abbey over at Starbucks. She asked why we hadn't sent her any clients over since the first. And her girls needed some more of our product to powder their noses. That's your end. You never missed a beat before and now you're screwing up. Big time screwing up, and it kinda gets me thinking. Then I stroll into Del Friscos and before you see me, I see you with some fed-looking guy, shaking hands. Ain't right. So I wait outside and follow him right back to the Roundhouse, and he greets some people and walks right in. I can *only* believe he's a cop. What the hell are you two doing together? The only conclusion I can draw is that you two guys are hooked up, working together, and I'm sure as hell not gonna be the last man standing."

Carl's face held the same gaze that it had until his injection took affect. Rick could sense he was trying to defend himself but was obviously unable to do so. His eyes caught the red glare of the clock, which had now entered the teens with fewer than fourteen minutes remaining. Carl wondered if the drug would have a lethal effect as time ran out or if it was a scare tactic to add shock value. One never knew with Rick.

Rick continued. "So you see, my *ex*-partner, it's gonna be you or me. We had it by the tail. Making money, mega connections, even a little power trip thrown in. It was us, all the way. And you pussied out, running to the feds to save your sorry little ass and bury mine. Unacceptable. Are you still with me, Carl?"

The clock read nine minutes left as he paused to add a little dramatic touch. Rick was enjoying this. That fact alone surprised even him. Who knew murder was such a fun profession?

Rick continued. "I spent the last several hours over at your place doing some tidying up. I dropped some notes down, which threatened us by an unsatisfied customer. Customer complaints for us are handled in a different manner than at Sears. Comprende, amigo? When the cops eventually look for you, they will discover that someone, other than me, had it in for you. It will look like you took the high road out of Dodge to save yourself, and I will make myself scarce for a time to give some validity to my fairy tale. I kinda like it. Well thought out and believable even to those inane guys who have you on their payroll."

Carl's mind was racing now, comprehending but not believing that he had been found out. He was careful to play both rolls but hadn't given Rick enough credit for his observations. Dumb luck. And he was going to pay for his mistakes with his life. Panic set in as these thoughts formed, and worse yet, his lack of ability to do anything about it. He was helpless, which was a trait he always vowed to avoid at all costs. Mentally his heart was beating out of his chest, but physically the drugs prevented it. A wave of overwhelming nausea consumed him, and he had to wonder if he became sick could he still vomit. The prospect of choking to death was so real he began to fear even more.

"I guess I said all I needed to, Carl. No reason to keep going over this point because all my conclusions have to be spot on. You messed up, old friend. I may never know what turned you, and I don't really give a rat's ass. I can fend for myself and scale down the service, and hey, won't have to split the profits. Think of it like a buyout. Good-bye, Carl. Hate to see it end this way, but you brought this on yourself, you self-serving bastard. Take the time you have left to reflect on all your mistakes, and don't forget this one. When I split, think of all the fun and opportunities out there for me and not for you. Hell, I might even miss you a little bit with all the history we had. Ah, maybe not."

With that thought, Rick removed the small clock from the roof and tossed it across the pavement until it rolled to a rest by Carl's left foot. Carl willed himself to look at the numbers. He waited for the motion to stop. But when it did, when it was at last close enough to read the numbers, the clock took one final roll. It was facedown.

Rick flashed his quirky, arrogant smile at Carl as he pulled open his door and slid behind the wheel. He never looked back.

He turned the ignition key and put the gear in reverse, slowly easing back to turn toward the down ramp. He slid his *Born to Run* CD into the player and accelerated. In less than one minute he was exiting the building.

Joey gave him a short salute as Rick passed the gate, which Joey then rolled shut before heading for the safety trailer across the street. At his next gaze in the side mirror, he could see a harmonic display of incendiary charges begin their explosive dances as the structure began to implode. *Good-bye,* he thought as his car shot down the incline toward the expressway.

"With tramps like us, baby we were born to run."

Chapter III

Rick's car drove down Chestnut Street, but not in the direction of his home. He slowed down as he neared the center of the block and came to a stop. As he reached for his door handle, it jerked open and a smiling attendant greeted him.

"How ya doing, Mr. Grosse?" asked Robbie the valet.

"Great, Robbie. You startled me when you opened the door. Guess my head was somewhere else."

Rick got out, and a tall, well groomed man pulled open the heavy door that led to the front hostess area in the Capital Grille. This was one of his favorite watering holes and eateries. The place was consistent; the staff knew his name and the steaks were fork tender. He found a seat at the bar, which was only partially occupied. To his right sat a middle-aged couple sipping martinis and sharing an order of Kobe Carpaccio. As she stabbed a piece, he noticed she had more rings on than the display case in Kay Jewelers. Her partner's piece looked like clumps of hair lying on the floor during a closing mop-up at any salon.

Jason the barkeep approached him and nodded. "The usual, Mr. Grosse?"

"Make it four fingers."

As soon as Jason started to pour, Rick's hand embraced the glass as the bronze colored liquid quickly rose in volume. He raised it to his lips and let the brandy pour into his mouth. He gulped rather than sipped, hoping it would take a little of the edge off. He had killed his oldest friend and partner only minutes earlier, and this was eating at him. He had never committed such a violent crime but at the same time knew it was a matter of survival. He would learn to live with it, just as he had with other traumatic instances that had been part of his past.

He ordered a dozen oysters on the half shell, which Jason soon pushed in front of him with a small bottle of Tabasco. Rick poured it over everything. He squeezed a shot of lemon wedge over everything. The fresh aroma of the ocean pleased him as the oyster slid over his taste buds, bringing the accompanying endorphin rush.

He went over a mental checklist in order to confirm he had covered his tracks that day. The two grand he had given to the regulars at his bimonthly poker game would pay for some of the alibi. Besides, he had won that last month, and he was just giving it back temporarily. Their tells were easy to spot, and he would have twice that back after a few more afternoons. Then there was Abbey, always reliable with enough cash or snuff. Carl's computer hard drive had been erased and no longer stored any pertinent information. A suitcase, clothes, and his toiletries were absent, hinting at a road trip. Even the current bills and mail were missing, indicating all personal matters were up-to-date. The thermostat had been set at sixty-eight degrees, reasonable for any May evening. The refrigerator was emptied of perishables, and no dirty dishes littered the sink. Carl was a bit anal when it came to neatness, reminding him of Felix Unger in the *Odd Couple*. It had all been covered, and to anyone who knew him it looked like a quick exit had been the order of the day.

As the next-to-last oyster lay exposed on his plate, Rick pointed to his empty glass, which was met with a nod from Jason. He liked this place. They made him feel important here. He was treated with respect. He liked to believe it was because of who he was and not the fact that he was a more than generous tipper. Either way, as he finished his second drink, most of the tension had exited his body, and he was beginning to feel like Rick again.

He glanced up at the large plasma TV, which graced each corner of the bar. The Phillies were down 7–4 to the Marlins, the lamest team in the division. It was only the eighth inning, and the Phillies were far from down and out. He was a Philly boy through and through. Countless days of his youth had been spent with his father on the third base line, idolizing Mike Schmidt. He bled Philly red and still attended home games when he needed to reminisce.

The bar was beginning to fill with the dinner crowd. He noticed two hot brunettes in Ann Taylor suits approach the bar, but his heart was not into the smooth operator mode he was so good at. Instead he watched as Ryan Howard took a third strike looking, stranding two men on in the bottom of the eighth.

"C'mon guys," he said to himself.

"One more for the road, Mr. Grosse?" Jason asked, breaking Rick's train of thought.

"I'm good, thanks," he replied. "Grab me the check when you get a minute, no rush."

It had been a long and tedious day. Tomorrow would be better. He would go home, pack, and check to make sure all of his proverbial ducks were in a row. His work was done and done well. He hated to screw up and would be damned if he would make any mistakes on a project this important.

Rick peeled a fifty and a twenty off his folded bills and dropped it on the bar.

"All you, Jason," he noted.

"Thanks Mr. G., that's very generous," he replied. The check was only half that and it *was* very generous. Jason beamed as Rick headed for the door and a much deserved dive into the sack.

CHAPTER IV

Rick's alarm sounded at 5:30 a.m., waking him to the sound of Philadelphia's Harold Melvin and the Bluenotes. The station doted their number one hit *The Love I Lost*. Rick loved that tune, but it brought back some sad memories. Seconds later his cell phone resounded with the generic ring that makes everyone in a room grab their cell phones to check their caller ID. Rick answered without checking the number.

"This better be good," he chided.

"Good morning, Mr. Rick, mon!" came the response from the caller. It was Claude, the manager of the timeshare resort that Rick would be arriving at later that afternoon. "All arrangements are in order. I will meet you at the airport at 1:30 and have that white Mustang convertible you desire. The room is spot on and the temperature is 81 degrees Fahrenheit, with the rich Caribbean sun at your service!"

Claude had a flare for details and would cater to those tourists who took care of him. Rick was one such customer. Rick liked that a lot, as it was the same way he took care of his clients. It kept them coming back, year after year.

Rick threw various toiletries in his bag and laid them next to his freshly pressed slacks, shirts, and shorts in his oversized suitcase. He didn't need anything too elegant as the island was known for its casual demeanor and slow pace, except for the one day twenty-six cruise ships dropped off loads of passengers. Its two big cities were to be avoided between eight a.m. and four p.m. when the streets were gridlocked with taxi cabs, outdoor vendors, and street hustlers all looking to make a buck. Tourists gawked in store windows as they filled their Carnival Cruise tote bags filled with mementos and tacky souvenirs for their envious friends at home. Some of the items truly were bargains. Dom Perignon came in around eighty bucks a bottle and Gentleman Jack topped out in the high teens. Swiss watches, designer jewelry, and the hottest electronics and cell phones were all at hand at a big savings. Haggling and price naming were to be expected, adding to the shopping experience as well as the comforting feeling that a soccer mom from Tennessee put one over on the local merchant. But the merchant thought the same thing.

Rick headed for the bathroom. He turned the heat lamp on and laid out his travel wardrobe. Light slacks, a short-sleeve shirt, and lace-less, slip-on shoes so as not to make passing through airport security any more of a hassle than it already was. He stripped off his boxers and entered the toasty bathroom. He stepped into the shower and felt the temperate stream of water caressing his body. He lathered his face and shoulders with a fierce motion as if washing away yesterday's events, which now eased from his body and soul. It felt good. Perhaps two steps ahead from being Lady Macbeth scrubbing her hands with the cry of "out damned spot" on her lips.

He stepped out of the warm mist and shut off the water. He picked up his favorite bath towel that a client from the west coast had given him. It was campy and gauche, which Rick liked. The towel was yellow and had a black outline of a body, mocking the chalk outline of a crime scene. The logo on the towel read **L.A. County Coroner's Office**. It always made him smile. Carl came to mind, but he knew there would never be an outline of his demise, buried under a mountain of stone and rubble. Shit happens.

Rick dressed and loaded the last few items into his carry on. The new Patterson book, his i-Pod, Bose headphones, and a U-shaped pillow for his neck were added to the bag. It would be a three-plus-hour flight to the Western Caribbean, and his inability to stay in one seat for that long tended to be problematic.

He placed two blue pills in his mouth and washed them down with the complimentary V-8 juice his fridge had been stocked with by his gracious partner. Nothing wrong with a little endorphin rush to wake up to. He grabbed the *Daily News* from the front stoop and turned the deadbolt on the door's upper lock. With his free hand he popped up his cell phone and punched in speed dial. Just as he put the phone to his ear, a black Lincoln town car pulled up in front of his residence. The driver door swung open and a man emerged dressed in a smart black Armani tux.

"Morning, Mr. Grosse," Jamal, his favorite driver, said.

"What's up, yo," Rick parried back in his natural Philly street slang.

Jamal popped the trunk and took Rick's bags. He put the large Pullman in first, laying it over the spare tire. The carry-on fit neatly next to it. He closed the trunk and circled the car, opening the rear passenger door for Rick. He pulled out down Locust Street and then made a right on Broad Street, which would bring him down toward I-95 and the final destination.

It was a twenty-minute ride to the Philadelphia International Airport. During the short ride, Rick flipped open his laptop and sent some business e-mails to various associates. He would be gone five days, and since Carl was no longer around, his workload almost doubled. He didn't mind. The first e-mail went out to Frankie "The Cheese" Romano. *Great moniker,* he thought. Why did all known associates have to have a middle nickname. Status, maybe? Frankie was putting together a small Atlantic City gathering for some made guys in New York and they needed some ladies, Cuban cigars, and party favors. Frankie didn't bother with details, which is where Rick and a bulk of his business came in. He was detail-oriented but not to the degree of being too anal. It worked for all involved. After expenses he would net a couple grand for an hour's worth of work.

Jamal pulled up to Terminal E, the overseas gate, which had been under new renovations for the past five years. Nothing was done quickly in Philadelphia thanks to a slow-running political machine. Jamal exited the driver's seat, popped the trunk, and carried Rick's bags to the edge of the curb.

"Enjoy, Mr. G.," Jamal said.

"Will do. Much needed, and the timing is right. Thanks." Rick stuffed a twenty into Jamal's hand and carried his bags to the counter.

The airport was not too crowded for a Saturday morning, which meant security wouldn't be a nightmare. US Air had direct flights on the weekend, which saved him time and the hassle of waiting in Charlotte or Miami. He would touch down by one thirty and be on his way.

He popped the second Xanax as he started feeling the effects of the first and headed down to the gate, looking for a quick bite. There was something about a pizza covered with scrambled eggs and cheddar cheese that seemed to go against such an American icon. He continued past the salt-drenched pretzels and the fast food staples, which he abhorred. Dining in an airport is a nutritional nightmare. If one is on a diet filled with high carbs, sodium, fat, and calories, then he's come to the right place. Proteins and vitamins are rare life forms in airport meals, unless found in a salad or fresh chicken breast not made of formed ground chicken. Rick settled on a cup of coffee and Nature Valley bar and then took a seat at gate 21.

As he started to doze off, a gruff female voice announced that the flight would be boarding in several minutes and no delays were expected. *"Those with young children, the elderly, and passengers with special needs will board first,"* the voice continued.

What is this, the fucking Titanic? Rick thought. His seat was in 2A, first class, so he would be comfortable for the three-and–a-half hour trip. Besides, with all those drugs and early cocktails in his system he would be well sedated within minutes after takeoff and wake up for the final descent.

Rick felt the landing gear emerging from the plane's underbelly with familiar grinding noises accompanying it. Greg, one of the plane's stewards, announced to the passengers to buckle up, as they would be touching down in several minutes (twenty minutes ahead of schedule).

As he peered out the window, Rick could see the strange sight that made landing in St. Maarten a unique experience. For starters, the flight path brought the plane in low, over an area filled with sunbathers, restaurants, and clusters of time shares. A chain link fence separated the airport from the masses. Here people would line up against the fence as the planes took off, waiting for the powerful blast of the turbos. The takeoffs were extreme at times, and the force would lift those against the fence as if they were born to fly—a head rush and a body rush free of charge. "Surfing the fence" was what locals called it. And since the bar was across from the runway, all warning signs went unheeded by the throngs of drunken thrill seekers.

CHAPTER V

One of the nicest things about landing at Princess Juliana International Airport is its size. There may be two to three dozen flights per day, and half of those are island hoppers, flying honeymooners to St. Barts or St. Kitts. Sometimes the impossible happens and luggage will be orbiting the carousel even before its owner is checked through customs, a truly remarkable feat of human ingenuity and hard work. Rick found his bag, and by the time he pulled the collapsible handle out, Claude was coming toward him with outstretched arms and a big grin.

"Ricky, mon, welcome home, and how was your flight?" Claude asked.

"No problem, mon!" Rick replied, mimicking the calypso singsong accent he so poorly imitated.

"The weather, she be gorgeous and your accommodations will be pristine shortly. Is your appetite worked up yet?"

"I'm famished, Claude, and I can use a Presidente. It's hard to find that beer in the states. How about if we shoot over to Lee's?"

"Not a problem. I parked across the lot, so give me your bags and we can head there and relax."

"All yours," Rick said.

As they drove away from the airport toward Lee's, a phantom taste of brandy burned across taste buds. This was the start of some well-needed rest and relaxation.

Both he and Claude sat out by the water and talked business to get it out of the way. Claude was instrumental in running Rick's small drug import operation. This kept them under the radar with authorities and larger cartels, both of which had a way of getting rid of the competition, and neither being busted by cops or butchered by rivals resulted in a storybook ending.

They dined on conch fritters and fresh snapper that had been removed from the sea by the multitude of fishermen employing their skills. The grill next to the bar emitted the smell of sweet baby back ribs and half chickens, another house favorite. The food was home cooked, better than reasonably priced, and filling. A perfect culinary trio. Rick reached into his pocket and removed his folded bills before Claude could do the same.

"Not this time, my friend," he said to Claude.

"Ah, but you pay me well, Rick, and you are a visitor to my island. It's—"

Rick cut him off mid-sentence, and Claude reached out to shake his hand for Rick's generosity.

"Your condo is all ready for you, Rick. The bar is stocked with your beverages of choice. Plenty of your brandy to go around! There is a case of beer and water in the refrigerator. Your Cuban cigars are fresh, and you can expect one of my employees to drop by and say hello around eight. Enjoy your evening, and we shall get together in a day or so. Ciao, my friend."

Rick pulled the keys from his pants pocket and drove back toward the airport, passing Maho Bay, and arriving at his condo moments later. A valet swung open the door and greeted him.

"Rick, mon, welcome home," Lawrence the valet crooned in a similar singsong island accent.

"Lawrence, mon, it always does my heart good to see you. Was that smile permanently attached to your face? Or is it that Claude pays you too much?"

The grin widened. Lawrence grabbed the luggage and led Rick up to his tenth-floor studio. Rick pulled out a twenty. Lawrence shook his head in a feigned attempt at a modest refusal and the twenty was shoved in Lawrence's top pocket. He held a thumb up and closed the door and left Rick in his island paradise.

Once inside, Rick stared out a thirty-foot clear glass wall that presented an unobstructed view, highlighted by the bluish-green tint of the Caribbean Sea. *Sunsets can be clichéd*, he thought, but tonight the sun appeared as a golden peach gently dipping its exterior into the tepid water. Actually, it even reminded him of the cover of his favorite Allman Brothers album. He turned away and approached the freestanding bar, where his next libation, Gentleman Jack, waited to be poured. He dropped one cube from the bucket into his glass and then fell back into the cushions of a recliner decorated in island motif. He closed his eyes and started to think about his life. It was not something he did too often. Usually he went on living in the hedonistic moment whenever possible. At times, though, he did reflect. How the hell did he become the person he was…? And was that so bad?

Chapter VI

Stephen Davis hopped up the steps as he approached the Roundhouse, Philadelphia's main police headquarters. Sitting on Seventh and Race, the circular four-story structure, is a dull concrete circle interspersed with windows covering the entire building. It is imposing but doesn't seem to fit into its surroundings, dwarfed by the Ben Franklin Bridge, which links New Jersey with Philly.

Davis entered the building and waited for the dank elevator to transport him to the top floor. The office of the Organized Crime Task Force, or OCTF, housed about a dozen members, all devoted to breaking up what was left of the once-powerful group that lived off the city and its vices. Davis was the team leader of four officers, each with different responsibilities and investigative expertise. His particular team was responsible for monitoring new scams and individuals trying to blend into the business community. He also had a number of confidential informants who were gathering hard-to-find street gossip.

He opened the door to his small office. It had two chairs, piles of memos, and the usual clutter that goes along with trying to do too much with too little. Two posters, nicely framed and dust free, graced the wall, which was about the only place in the office that was dust free. One poster featured Robert De Niro facing off against Chazz Palmeteri, a NY skyline looming beneath them, and large red letters stating *A Bronx Tale*. To its left hung the classic *Goodfellas* poster, which featured the silhouettes of Ray Liotta and Joe Pesci staring off into opposite directions. Too much De Niro might be considered overkill. Those movies not only reinforced his mission to the city but gave him a wealth of quotes, which the rest of his workmates were now used to.

He was predictable at times. "*Is it better to be loved or to be feared?*" was one of Davis's favorite quotes and had became so played out, it had lost its meaning.

Ellen Sue Diamond strode into his office looking as sexy as ever. She was medium height with her hair just slightly permed, giving her the look of a model strutting down the runway. She had pure beauty, which was a bright light in an otherwise dull, depressing environment. She was also quite intelligent, graduating from Temple and getting a master's degree in accounting. She was the squad's forensics accountant, being able to trace a money trail better than ET did with Reese's Pieces. Her most recent case involved a major scam artist who was embezzling money from his friends and family for a nonexistent business. None of his investors were aware of his serious addiction to craps and Pai Gow poker. In the classic pyramid scheme, he would use the new money to pay off his first investors and so on down the line. But his losses far outweighed his gains, and he panicked in the end. He killed his wife for her half-million dollar insurance policy but neglected to realize that his fingerprints appeared on her neck two days after postmortem. In his cellar Ellen Sue found documents adding up his debts on a single page. Not the smartest crook. The second page showed his future assets, which were mainly made up of insurance policies and the expected proceeds from the sale of his dead wife's antique doll collection. Raggedy Ann turned out to be one of the prosecution's star witnesses. Life without parole had been the jury's verdict.

The other lovely team lady was Ashley Stone, the case-cracking beauty who occasionally served as Davis's love interest. A breath of clean air in an often stuffy office, Ashley was instrumental in finding the aforementioned postmortem prints. She was just as dangerous with a microscope and bacterial culture as with her gun during an executed search warrant.

Then there was Gerald Eckland. He was the computer expert with a full repertoire of electronic know-how that would rival top technicians at IBM. He was good-natured except when it came to his nickname which he abhorred. Alex Rodriguez is called A-Rod. Jennifer Lopez is J-Lo. When Davis combined Eckland's first and last name, he came up with Geek, a name that fit him to a tee. On the contrary, Geek was well-read and well-traveled. He was quite fluent in Spanish and street slang and an avid Phillies historian who could also play a mean harp. Eckland, Diamond, Stone, and Davis together made up the core of the team. The result was a high-closing case percentage and a great deal of respect in the Roundhouse.

Ellen Sue peeked her head around the corner of his office entryway. "Davis, have you had contact with Carl yet? He was supposed to check in with us yesterday evening at some time or another."

"Ask Geek," he said. "He was the last to be in touch with him."

Carl had become an informant after screwing up. He was pulled over on a traffic stop and found with a gun he had no permit for and claimed not to own. The team took the opportunity to nail him, especially when they ran it through ballistics and the gun matched a four-year-old hit on Victor "The Beef" Carpaccio in South Philly. He'd been shot as he stepped out of Il Guardino after a night of celebrating an Eagles four-point loss to Seattle after being a ten-point favorite.

None of the team believed Carl had anything to do with the murder, but he'd been left holding the bag. Carl didn't do killings. He may have acquired the piece, but they knew he didn't pull the trigger. Their bluff paid off, and they could now use him to bust the elusive Rick Grosse, who they believed had moved on to bigger crimes. They knew Grosse had set up some drug connections with the Columbians and would protect the routes, which guaranteed safe passage to Philly. His numerous trips to the Caribbean were a telltale sign, as was his increased spending habits and growing bank accounts. Carl had handled the day-to-day activities and the catering to their wealthy clientele, but Rick was the major bread winner and hustler. Carl's assignment was to copy all the files on the hard drive as well as any papers that could lead to those higher on the food chain than himself.

Davis picked up his cell and speed-dialed Carl's number. The call rang twice and went through to voice mail. Now he was concerned. Over the next two hours of endless office work, all twenty calls went to voice mail.

He yelled into the outer office, "Geekman, did you place the GPS in Michael's phone, or what?"

"You betcha!" he replied.

"Don't you know he aint picking up?" Davis said.

"I'll get right on it, boss." Geek connected the jack from his laptop to the cell phone and pulled up the screen showing a street map of the city. He pressed in a unique, three-digit code and a red pulsating dot appeared. It was centered in an alley behind the southwest corner of the Philadelphia Zoo. He switched screens to get a zoomed-in satellite view of his target. Instead of the bipedal smudge of a human he intended to see, what appeared was a pile of debris that covered the street.

Shit, he thought. This was the area that was being added to the zoo to create a safari exhibit, the site of an old parking structure the city had deemed unsafe. Was it possible that under the mountain of concrete, Carl lay buried? *Electronics don't lie,* he thought. *Unless a monkey is crapping on the program.*

"Uh, boss? I think I found Carl, and it's not a pretty sight from seven miles above. We gotta roll."

The team piled into the Bronco and affixed the strobing cherry to the side of the roof. It would be a fifteen-minute ride during late morning. Davis grabbed his radio and requested the canine squad meet them at the site with two cadaver dogs. He then called the forensics team in their squad, just in case.

As they approached the site, a crew was in the process of removing the debris from the old structure. Since the demolition had happened yesterday, they obviously hadn't gone too far down. Geek removed his computer and retyped the code with additional digits. The new code would give a measurement in feet rather than miles. The pulse was still there, and the distance was reading fourteen feet. As he waited for the system to calibrate further they were met by Lt. Ray's group. He had the dogs, medical emergency equipment, and the crime scene kit. Davis hurriedly approached him the site foreman.

Ellen Sue took out her wallet and flipped it open to expose her credentials.

"What can I help you with, lady?" he shouted. He waved his hand to stop the crew so he could hear her.

"Detective Diamond," she said. "We have a tip from a reliable source that this may be a crime scene. Since I left my X-ray goggles at home, we need your help."

"No problem, I have natural X-ray vision, but I need to change into my cape first, ma'am." He chuckled.

No sense in trying to humor this guy, she thought. "Would you feel better if I said we received an anonymous call that there may be a body buried here and we need your crew to clear the pile over here, where the dogs are picking up the scent and that any delays or added cost will be picked up by the city? Or should I just slap you with the court order in my hand and tell you to get off my crime scene before I throw you in jail. Your pick."

"Lady, no problem. But if the city's gotta pay for it, the politicians are just gonna add another tax. We gotta clear it anyways," he commented. He waved his right arm and pointed with his left, directing the crew to dig over where he was indicating.

The hoe dumped the heavy stone into the claw of the crane and it was loaded into a waiting receptacle. The dogs' barking grew in intensity. Geek redialed Carl's number on his phone. This time they all heard the faint ring.

After several more minutes, noticeable red stains appeared on the larger cement pieces. Two arms secured together at the wrists appeared next. Further excavation was halted until the crime team could arrive. Carl would no longer be calling in. Now they had a homicide. Carl had been murdered under their watch, and as a leader, Davis did not take the death of his key witness lightly. For him, it was personal.

Chapter VII

Rick's first thought focused on some youthful experiences. His childhood had been okay, he thought. He remembered his neighborhood and his father. They called his dad the "bartender du jour" because he was the block's resident mixologist. He was not an alcoholic by any stretch, but on the weekends he was known to get drunk. Rick avoided thoughts on those times since his father's unpredictable behavior created dark places in his memories. He and his sister would go down to the corner stoop and just hang out with their friends. No good would ever come when his dad had too much. Yet he never saw him strike his mother, nor would he get violent. He just got stupid. So Rick escaped by trying to get away with things and by taking advantage of situations and crossing the limit.

He had promised himself never to spend everything and to save nothing, another trait he shared with his father. His father always had to have the newest of everything, such as cars, stereo equipment, and various other *status* items. One year, the family's limited savings were depleted. The air conditioning unit, heating unit, and roof all needed repairs. The household budget was drastically trimmed, a necessity Rick and his sister didn't appreciate.

That would never happen to him.

He brought the glass of brandy up to his lips and took a large gulp.

His thoughts then turned to Brandi. Brandi McHugh, the girl who stole his heart and disappeared. The girl who made him drink her name. A smile graced his mouth. They had first met in high school when Jake Westy had come to Philly, down I-95 from Brooklyn. Being the new kid on the block, Jake immediately set out to impress, not just the ladies but the guys. The first time she met Ricky, he and Brandi had been talking during break. Jake approached with this tough guy attitude and told Ricky to get lost. Bad comment. Rick applied a closed fist to Jake's genitals. As Jake doubled over, his face was greeted by Ricky's right jab, catching him squarely on the nose. The end result was a crimson flow from his nose, and the necessity of a dentist visit. Two of his front teeth were missing in action.

"Don't fuck with me or Brandi. Either go back to Brooklyn or fall in line. You are messing with the wrong guy."

It would be the first and last encounter between the three. From then on, Brandi and Ricky were a couple. They would spend free time at school and in the city together. They recognized each other's touch, emotions, and bodies. Two were one. In the summer of 1982, senior year, it all crumbled. Brandi got pregnant and her parents' strict Catholic values made them move away. She was forbidden to have any contact with Rick, and she didn't. Her parents' rules were so strong she eventually was convinced that Rick was pure evil. Her love faded. His did not. It soured him, not only in regard to women but his outlook as well. He would never let anyone influence what he did or what he thought. If he wanted something or someone he would go after it. Selfishness and ego took over his actions.

He opened his eyes and shook his head back and forth. Too much thinking and too much hurt were beginning to encompass his thoughts. He raised his glass, downing the copper-colored salvation, and got up. It was all he had left of her—memories and booze.

Almost at the same instant he stood, a soft knock came from the door. Rick crossed the room and slowly opened it.

"Good evening, Mr. Grosse. I am Esperanza, Claude's friend," she said with a smile.

"Rick, call me Rick, please."

"Are you going to let me in? I cannot squeeze through that small opening."

The door opened, and Esperanza strode past him toward the bar. "I helped Claude get your place just as you like it. I hope I pleased you, Rick."

"It's better than ever," he said, his mind and gaze fixed on her.

She was a raven-haired beauty with shoulder-length hair and a light tan complexion. Her proportioned stature had him mesmerized. Her round breasts fit perfectly into her skimpy, crimson-colored dress, and her tight calves accented her come-fuck-me footwear.

"What shall I make for you? Claude told me that brandy was your drink of choice, or was he telling me a little white lie?" she whispered.

"Claude is as honest as the day is long, and he told you the correct choice." He came closer, his voice low and husky. "But for now, let's forget about Brandi."

She raised an eyebrow devilishly and grabbed the bourbon. She poured several fingers of his drink into a highball glass. She then added one cube. Next she took a tall glass, walked to the freezer, and poured an equal amount of Ketel One into hers. No ice was necessary.

Rick strode over to the large plush wicker couch and sat on the middle cushion. Without any prodding, Esperanza followed and slowly slid on the adjoining cushion. She ever-so-slightly rubbed against his thigh.

Rick glanced over and saw that her nipples had a slight peak to them and then stated, "Would you like me to turn down the air conditioner a little because ..." He let his voice trail, expecting the meaning to be obvious.

She stopped him in mid-sentence and teased, "I see you are very observant. I will take that as a compliment that you like what you see. And no thanks, it's comfortable." She smiled.

Rick took a sip of his drink. He then took the gold tube that held his favorite cigar and twisted it open. He removed it and twirled it around between his thumb and first two fingers and then slid it between his lips.

Esperanza watched and took a sleek gold lighter from her purse, swirling the wheel and offering him a light.

"Thank you," he said and slowly inhaled, the tip burning a soft orange hue.

"My deepest pleasure," she gently responded. She then stood up and took his cigar. She pursed it between her lips, inhaling its fragrant smoke. Exhaling, she blew two smoke rings in a skyward path and then sent the next two down between his legs in a suggestive manner. His mind flicked back to Brandi. It was difficult not to compare women he had sex with to the woman he considered his soul mate. Often times it was Brandi's name he screamed and her hair he grasped in the fever of his mind.

"I see you are hoisting the mast," she said in a playful, observant manner.

Rick said nothing as his body began reacting to her ministrations. She sat on his lap facing him, her firm breasts protruding below his shoulders. She slowly moved her hips in a circular motion, feeling him pushing up against her. She next grabbed the straps on her dress and lifted it up over her shoulders in a slow, purposeful motion. Rick's hands automatically circled her as his fingers disengaged the lone clasp of her bra. His lips headed for one of her breasts, covering it with his mouth. His teeth gently brushed against it before he bit her nipple, hard enough to startle her but soft enough to excite her. Esperanza let out a soft, pleasured moan as he varied the intensity of his playfulness. Their eyes met as the only sound in the room was the growing intensity of their breathing.

Esperanza then slid off of his lap and perched on the area rug between his knees. She slowly unbuttoned the clasp of his shorts and lowered the zipper, freeing his imprisoned, throbbing muscle. She then slid it through the slit in his boxers and gently covered it with her soft lips. Her hand then slid up and down in an even cadence. Her lips and tongue licked and circled him, brushing him between her teeth, against her cheeks, and down her throat. Rick's moans increased with each of her movements. His body intermittently trembled as the pleasure she conveyed made him tingle.

"You've been pretty quiet these past several moments," she teased. "Am I doing this right, am I missing anything?"

Rick just shook his head, lost in the moment of pure carnal pleasure. She then stood up, sat back on his lap, and guided him into her. She moved first, and then he followed her lead. They moved as one, their breathing synchronized. Seconds later they exploded as one, orgasms in perfect harmony. They trembled, bringing harmonic smiles to their faces. Esperanza let out a deep breath as she dismounted him, her weak legs barely making it to the couch. She turned toward him, her mouth surrounding him and gently sucking on his lower lip. Their tongues danced around their warm mouths, ending almost a minute later.

"That was fucking amazing," Rick whispered.

"That *was* fucking amazing," she mimicked.

They reclined back and sighed together. Rick picked up his drink and cigar. She pulled out a cigarette from her purse and leaned in as Rick was lighting his. She guided his fist toward the tip of her Marlboro Light, her cheeks hollowing as she deeply inhaled. Her lips parted as a creamy ball of smoke emerged, only to be taken back in her mouth as if sucking his cock. She sipped her vodka, inhaling again as the smoke curled over her lips in a fluent stream. Rick was still enchanted by her pure sexuality.

"Why has Claude been hiding you for so long?" he murmured.

"He hasn't," she answered. "I recently arrived from Costa Rica. We met and then Claude was so impressed with my brains and beauty, he offered me a job."

"That makes two of us you have impressed, and since you are working for him, in a roundabout way you are working for me."

"Uh oh," she joked. "I hope I am not in any sort of trouble for sleeping with the boss."

They both laughed together and finished their cocktails.

CHAPTER VIII

Davis turned the Bronco in the direction of 321 S. University Avenue, home of the medical examiner's offices. He would let the forensics team gather all the information they could. Realizing the crime scene had been so compromised by the garage demolition, the team would be busy for some time examining the area around the victim, taking photographs, and bagging any materials that may have contained fingerprints or any DNA evidence.

When they arrived, Carl's body had just been deposited on the stainless steel table. The manila tag laced around his large toe would be burned into Davis's memory. Sonny in *A Bronx Tale* would always say, *"Nobody cares."* Well, Davis did.

About an hour into the autopsy, Ashley Stone popped her head in the room with her usual overly energetic movements. "I've got something here for you, Davis," she said.

"Animal, vegetable, or mineral?" he taunted back.

"Mineral."

"I can't stand the suspense."

Ashley was a rarity—a combination or energy, beauty, and brains. She was not only part of the Organized Crime Task Force but Davis's occasional lover. Against all odds they kept it secretive and discreet, a difficult task within their confines. She produced a small folded envelope, which contained a shell casing found at the crime scene.

"I'm going to check it out under the scope and then swab it for any DNA trace. Hopefully it will give us something. May take two days but it may also give us some kind of lead."

She hopped back to the lab and began to process it. Wearing latex gloves so as not to contaminate the sample she removed the shell casing from the clear white envelope. Stone took the casing and placed it under the lens of her high-powered Cannon microscope. She examined the oily ridges along the bronze casing, the result of loading the clip. Nothing promising appeared but she snapped high resolution photos so they could be entered in the AFIS system, where all fingerprints taken of those who had passed through the system were housed. If a match with ten points of similarity occurred, it could be a slam dunk, although that was rarely the case. Davis would surely reward her with her exotic desires if it were, so she crossed her fingers and her legs in the hope that big number ten would appear in the database.

She then tore open a plastic wrapper that housed a six-inch cotton applicator stick. Next she added alcohol to the swab and gently ran it over the exterior of the casing. She then snipped off the stick about an inch below the cotton and transferred it to a waiting bullet-shaped centrifuge tube. She swiveled her chair and inserted the tube into the circular opening of the machine and set the spinning timer for the desired minutes. Although the DNA results would take several days, she wanted the results a week ago.

In the basement of the Roundhouse, Jim Kelley was in the ballistics lab trying to match the second shell casing with the weapon that had fired it. He was the youngest fringe member of the team and was on loan from Quantico, getting some field experience as part of his FBI requirements. He was twenty-eight and single but not for long. He was getting married in two weeks to the girl who had been his college sweetheart at Boston College from day one. They had met in a bookstore on Commonwealth Avenue in Newton. They had both been reaching for the last shelved copy of a textbook that was required reading for their criminal psychology course. Both had been focused on grabbing the remaining copy, oblivious to their surroundings. When their hands touched the binding and their gazes met, it was over. Their story had all the makings of a successful Hollywood chick flick.

The door to the lab swung open, and Ashley approached as Jimmy was removing his protective goggles.

"No luck her with any prints yet?" she asked.

"I'm making a little headway on my end. My guess is this came from a Glock .38. The tip is pretty beat up. It probably smashed into the concrete from a short distance, fewer than ten feet. Now we just have to run all of those models purchased from all tri-state dealers. And then, in ten years, we'll have our perpetrator," he mused glumly.

Ashley smiled. She knew this was where hard work and luck would be much needed. She turned to Jimmy and asked, "So when's the big day? I know it's soon."

"Two more weeks, and I'll be a new man." He grinned.

"Hey, Kelley, did you know scientists just discovered a food that decreases a woman's sex drive by 95 percent?" she asked.

"No way! Tell me so I can make sure it's avoided at all costs." His gullibility was unfathomable.

"It's called 'wedding cake.' Good luck!" And with that dig she turned back toward the door.

His resounding ha-ha-ha followed her out.

As the autopsy progressed, there were few promising results. The weight and gravity of the structure kept little of what remained of Carl intact. His skin was missing and parts of his bones had been pulverized into splinters by the force. The skull was surprisingly intact, but examination showed no bullet holes or fragments.

"Just one atomic case of blunt force trauma," the examiner noted. "We can run a toxicology screen if we find any tissue, and if there are any surfaces that may attract some prints, we'll check that too. Don't count on anything, Davis."

It had been a long morning and afternoon, and the evening would probably follow suit. It would be several more days before the blast area could be finally cleared. There would be piranhas of the press jamming them up with speculation and questions. Because Carl's business activities touched upon so many people, including those who didn't like to answer questions, the enormous task of solving this case was just beginning. A liquid dinner might be in order.

Davis turned in to one of his favorite nondescript bars, which dotted the area around the Warwick Hotel, and ducked into a corner booth. It was *his* corner booth for thinking and planning his next steps. He removed a small spiral notebook from his coat and opened it to a blank page. He smiled to himself. His notebook was inspired by the old Peter

Falk *Columbo* reruns he sat riveted to in his teens. His superstition was that the book was actually a crime-solving tool for the TV star, so he adapted it to his style. If it wasn't in the book, it wasn't solvable. If it wasn't solvable, write it in the book, and a guilty party magically appeared.

He wrote his plans first. They needed to trace all phone calls from the past several days and compare them with his known business connections and friends. *Unless he used a disposable cell for those calls,* Davis jotted down. Next Davis scribbled bank records, credit card receipts, and maybe EZ pass tolls and videos in case his car sported one such device. *Gun permits?* What really bothered Davis was how Carl had wound up in such a desolate and gated location. *Was it a meet? Maybe it was business transaction? Was it a setup, or was he taken against his will and brought there?* He figured it was probably the latter.

As he kept jotting notes, he denoted names of his team to investigate each individual part of the whole puzzle. With the most obliterated crime scene he had ever witnessed, maybe it was time to draw Lt. Columbo out of retirement. Shit, he did have a 100 percent crime solving rate. He pounded down his final shot of Bullet bourbon, threw a twenty down on the table, and called it a night.

CHAPTER IX

Rick stirred from beneath his silk sheets, which were all that was left of his formerly well-made bed. He was mentally and physically drained, but the latter was caused by his own volition. He smiled, recounting the wonderful pleasures he had experienced the night before. It had been two days ago that he'd killed Carl and could only assume he was still just a missing person. The American newspaper that circulated on the island, the *International Tribune*, only carried major news stories interspersed among local ads and events. The *New York Times* and *LA Times* might be found, but they too would be of no consequence. The *Philadelphia Daily News* would not be a renowned tabloid unless you liked thirty-seven pages about Philadelphia sports, sixty-five pages of ads, and three pages of local homicides and bank robberies. It did have a colorful cover with catchy headlines, like when a distraught stock broker jumped from a twenty-story building and the headline read **Man versus Sidewalk; Sidewalk Wins.** Gruesome, but kind of catchy.

He emerged from the sheets and headed for the kitchen area. The cold floor alternated with the warm tiles, heated through the open window of the midmorning sun. He opened the fridge and removed a carton of passion fruit nectar, unpeeled the plastic circular cap, and washed down his morning wake up of vitamins and a another Xanax. He poured a shot of Appleton Estate rum and sank into the couch. His mind was in vacation mode. Thought of last night's erotica with Esperanza were still fresh as a faint hint of her fluids remained on his chest.

His mind quickly traveled back to his youth. He hadn't seen his sister in several years and felt a tinge of guilt. She was a mirror image of their mother, studious, reliable, and resourceful. She finished high school with no real desire to peruse a career that required a prolonged education, so their mother enrolled her in a culinary program outside Atlantic City, and she excelled. Her interests gravitated toward a combination of ethnic cuisines, entertainment, and business. Her goal was to set up a catering business for those with a more adventurous and trendy palate. Where better to start a small catering business than in the decadent hills of Los Angeles? Along the way she met Anthony Mendicino, a sharp and creative North Jersey native with a flair for light Italian creations and artistic desserts. And besides, he was hot. They focused on their studies and after graduation were set up outside Burbank where they plied their trade. His brother-in-law's father had some connections on the coast, and within several years they were firmly implanted as sous chefs to the stars. They eventually married and the distance grew between Rick and his sister.

Maybe it was last night's passion, but Brandi had again eased back into his thoughts. During Thanksgiving of their senior year in 1985, the couple drove down the Atlantic City Expressway for a weekend of partying. A buddy's father had gotten them a room for two nights at Resorts and tickets for the Police.They pulled up to the valet, exited his RX-7, and he tipped the attendant twenty dollars. It not was only to impress Brandi with his money but also so he might be remembered for the "big tip" from the "young, straggly kid." To this day he was still known as a generous tipper.

The bellman wheeled their bags in as the couple walked over to the registration desk. They were given two plastic cards. They handed one to the bellman and followed him into the elevators, and they exited at the top floor. He and Brandi glanced at each other and smiled. They proceeded down the hall where their door was opened and the luggage placed on the strapped luggage caddy. Another twenty appeared, this one gracing the bellman's open palm. He smiled, nodded, and exited the room to give them privacy.

Rick remembered Brandi drawing the large paisley curtains and staring out at the grayish-blue Atlantic. They embraced at the vista, exchanging passionate kisses, the ones that stay with you for an eternity, the ones that define a moment.

He remembered the blast they'd had that evening. They gambled on the slots, even winning several hundred dollars, which he gave her. They flashed fake IDs at the cocktail waitresses and drank shots of tequila. They strolled on the boardwalk before the concert, stealing drags off the joint he had brought. The energy of the concert took them even higher. They sang, laughed, and enjoyed every second with each other. It was like nothing outside their world existed.

As they headed back to the room, they exchanged verbal and physical taunts that heightened their playfulness. Arriving at the room, Ricky slid the key into the door, and as they both reached for the handle, a sensual shiver shot through him. As their eyes met at this moment, he knew she was feeling it too. As he recalled now, it was another one of those defining moments. The night was filled with passionate, unselfish lovemaking, what seemed to him to be another level. They laughed, moaned, and hugged. They came as one, their bodies in a rhythmic dance of pure pleasure.

Esperanza's fluidity had been close to that, but was it close enough?

Rick's reminiscing was jarred by the ring of his cell phone. He clicked the green button and held the phone up to his ear.

"Good morning, Rick." Claude spoke cheerily into the phone.

"Good morning back at you, my friend."

"You sound well this morning. I am assuming Esperanza sufficiently welcomed you back last evening."

"Never a finer host has graced this island paradise," Rick retorted.

"Listen, my friend; we will meet in Marigot, say noon for lunch and business if it suits you."

"What time is it now?"

"Half past eight. Is that okay?"

"Yes. I'll meet you at our favorite place."

"Later then, my friend." And Claude was gone.

Rick turned off the phone and set it down on the table. He rose, stripped off his boxers, and headed to the shower. Rick wondered why his memories were filling his mind. Maybe it was last night's encounter. Perhaps his intermittent curiosity about his first love was meant to return to his thoughts during unsure times. Hell, maybe he just really missed her and drinking shots named after her wasn't as conducive to forgetting her as he hoped. Whatever; these thoughts were occurring on a more frequent basis, and he may never understand why. Maybe it was a premonition of things to come.

He stepped out of the shower and dried off before running the dryer through his thinning brown hair. He half smiled at the mirror in approval before quickly changing and grabbed his keys. Time for a quick cup of coffee, a smoke, and the start of his day.

He drove the twisting roads down to Simpson Bay and parked his Mustang in front of the tiny pink French patisserie next to the local convenience store. He entered the shop, which was filled with the sweet aroma of chocolate croissants and fruit-filled muffins. He ordered a savory crepe filled with mushrooms, spinach, and a delicate béarnaise sauce. Rick savored every bite. It was to die for. He was not a "foodie" by definition but loved good authentic food. When he was halfway done, he went next door and picked up a Miami *Herald*. It was opening weekend, and the Phillies were facing the Marlins.

He sat down, turned to the sports news, and finished his breakfast. Dessert was a cup of espresso and a Marlboro. A feast for a king. Scanning the paper, he saw that pitcher Cliff Lee had shut out the Marlins.

Life was good.

He hopped back into the Mustang and released a latch. The top retracted, exposing the fire-engine red interior. He connected the i-Pod, and his modern-age mix tape beamed out from the six speakers.

He drove by the airport and the inclining one-lane road through Cupecoy. He parked by the horseshoe-shaped marina filled with high end shops, duty free bargains, and bistros. He grabbed a case of beer and a couple of Cubans, tossed them into his trunk, and headed toward his rendezvous with Claude.

Claude sat out on the small passageway that served as extra seating several feet from the surrounding boat slips. The midday sun reflected off the water, adding several degrees to the warm climate. He waved to get Rick's attention and gestured to the chair across from him.

"Good afternoon, my friend," Claude said and smiled. "It's been a year since your last visited, and I would like to fill you in on what's been happening here."

Rick held up his hand and summoned the waiter. "Knob Creek, a double," he told the waiter. "Please continue, Claude."

Claude began. "We do a little business together. A little coke, which I get up to the states. A few thousand cigars and various contraband, which you have difficulty finding because of your government's tightened security since the unfortunate disaster. I appreciate our business. I have expanded my activities here since then." Claude handed a pair of binoculars to Rick and told him to focus to the left of a large cruise ship sitting at the dock. "My partners take a fishing boat out once a week in the general vicinity of the ship and actually catch some fish. They also drop several tightly wrapped packages of powder into a designated area at a given time. Some of the stewards on the ship take their long hooks and pull them into range so they may be captured. These stewards are paid handsomely."

Rick noticed all of this happening as Claude narrated the scene.

"You have this down to a science," Rick commented.

"Yes I do. I thought you might be interested in expanding your business, Rick. You needn't give me an answer now, but I just thought it might be a consideration."

For the next several minutes Claude detailed how the product was taken safely off the ship and deposited at certain locations. It was safe and foolproof, and no transactions had been discovered. What Claude was seeking was a bigger customer base, and he knew Rick had the right connections in the states.

What he didn't know was that Rick would soon be a person of interest in a recent case in Philadelphia.

And at this point, neither did Rick.

CHAPTER X

Davis's alarm blared out *"I Got You Babe"* at 6:15 a.m. on Friday morning. *Groundhog Day,* he mused, the eternal song that started every day of Bill Murray's hellish existence as he waited for groundhog Puxatawny Phil to make his annual prediction. He quickly shut off the music and hoped it wasn't going to be one of *those* days.

He preformed his morning ritual of shaving in the shower, running a brush through his hair, and a thirty second aberration of brushing his teeth. He slid on his Dockers, ripped the plastic layer off his recently captured dry cleaning, and slid into his shirt. He wanted to get in early, so he grabbed a bottle of water, swallowed his multivitamin, and left for the station.

Traffic was light from his Spring Garden apartment, several blocks from the Art Museum. It was about a twenty-block ride, and life's good when it's a ten-minute drive to work.

He pulled the Bronco into his designated spot and scampered up to the Roundhouse two steps at a time. He was confident that some of the forensics and more autopsy results would be available today. He was on a mission to solve this case, and his tenacity was apparent in his demeanor. He nodded to some of the uniforms sipping their Wawa coffee on the plaza and headed to his fourth-floor office.

As he left the elevator, Marcy handed him several manila folders, which he hoped contained some of his expected reports. He was the first to arrive, which was his goal. He liked the peace and privacy of having some alone time in order to organize his thoughts. Once his mind started racing and his ADD kicked in, he was all over the board.

Ellen and Geek knew this and were great interpreters of his random thoughts and ramblings.

He opened the first folder, which contained the ME's preliminary findings.

Name:	Carlson Mickels
Date:	April 28, 2011
Examiner:	Evan Gandalf, MD
D.O.B.	August 10, 1965
Age:	46
Race:	Caucasian
Sex:	Male
Case#:	03297291-2011
Investigator	Philadelphia homicide, OCTF Bureau
External Findings:	Body was discovered in a building recently demolished on April 27, 2011. Body was located and delivered here. Victim was wearing what appears to be a navy blue sport coat and ivory dress shirt. The body was severely traumatized with multiple separations of bone and tissue fragments found. No entry or exit wounds have been found on the remains examined thus far. Visible abrasions are evident on the skin layers, but no determination can be made when they occurred around time of death. More examinations will follow.
Internal Findings:	Blood levels produced an elevated reading of alcohol with a reading of 1.4 percent. There were traces of the metal Rocuronium Bromide at levels not found in a normal sample. The skeletal system was destroyed by the traumatic impact and is inconclusive. The same holds true with the gastrointestinal, urinary, and central nervous systems, which will be examined if possible.
Conclusion:	Death was caused by severe impact to the head and spinal column. The existence of the above mentioned foreign chemical found in the toxicology screen was not found to be a contributing factor to death but may have caused death at a later time if the trauma had not occurred first. It is therefore this office's conclusion that cause of death was homicide and an investigation should begin immediately.

Davis's mind began to race as he jotted down notes. *The report said the victim was either drugged prior to or after he had been transported to building. Why was the substance injected? How easy or hard is it to obtain this drug? Are there any other cases on file that have a similar MO? Who would want to kill him and why? Need to closely examine site for any documents or personal belongings as to where he was. Who was the last to see him? Known enemies?* He continued to write and filled several pages with pressing questions.

He was startled as Ellen and Geek strode into the office.

"Good morning, boss," Ellen bellowed, noticing he was transfixed on a file.

After nearly launching from his chair, he exchanged pleasantries and motioned them both to sit. He filled them in on what he'd read before they even moved.

"This file just came in, and it's quite bizarre. As we assumed, this was no accident, but we have a unique twist." He explained the toxicology report, and their expressionless faces grew puzzled. He grabbed the three remaining files and handed one to each of them.

"I haven't examined these yet, so let's meet back in an hour and compare notes. We'll meet in conference room B in an hour."

Geek strode to his desk and glanced at the white tab on the folder. It read *Full Service Concierges,* the name of Carl's business venture. He knew it was one of their top priority investigations. The report gave a brief description of Carlson Michael and Ricky Grosse's enterprise, which included ticket scalping, the escort services, and their most widely used hotels and contacts in Atlantic City. He wrote in the margin. The company had been investigated in several car bombings involving several influential rival mobs, which may tie in to the demolition aspect. He read on and gathered notes.

Ellen Sue sat at her desk and opened her folder. It was filled with financials that included recent credit card transactions and bank statements. The bank statements were ordinary. They contained mortgage and utility payments and the basic ATM withdrawals. She read on and noticed the credit card activities were linked to some known offshore gambling sites as well as several repetitive hotel stays. Tedious detective work, but maybe they had some significance. There was a pattern. Carl had become an informant several months ago, but at first sight it looked as if he was still carrying on some of his business with Ricky. Notes in her distinctive red Sharpie were beginning to fill the margins.

Davis was scanning the list of calls made within seventy-two hours of Carl's demise. He would have to cross-reference the numbers, but he recognized the calls to Ricky's cell. A flurry of calls had been made up until midnight prior to the demolition, and then they all ceased. *Were they made to set up a meet?* He would check with the phone company to see which cell towers the calls had bounced off. Maybe he could link Ricky to a specific location and then bring him in for questioning. He had nothing to haul his ass in yet, but Ricky was the obvious person of interest. His gut told him that.

The morning flew by as each of them studied the files and developed alternative theories about what had happened, why it happened, and who may have been responsible for the homicide.

The trio headed down to Chinatown for lunch. They arrived at Sang Kee Duck House and were greeted by Yan, their favorite waiter. Ashley Stone had rushed from the lab to meet them.

They crossed a small opening and headed to a rear window table. The menus were presented, which was unnecessary as they all knew it as well as repeating the Miranda Rights. It was going to be a working lunch. They all ordered roast pork and noodle soup and an order of vegetable dumplings. The usual.

"Grosse is out of the country," Davis said. "Homeland Security verified he flew out between the time of death and the discovery of the body. Judge Chambers is granting us a search warrant due to their relationship as partners. I'm still working on getting the cell phone records and recent bank transactions for the past several days."

"I think we need to pull him in when he lands at the airport," Ellen said. "It will catch him off guard, and maybe we can get something. He's scheduled to arrive on Sunday. The airlines will monitor the passenger manifestos in case there is a change of plans. We need to check his car to see if there's any debris from the crime scene on the tires or undercarriage. He's our best suspect, and if he found out about Carl's role, he's definitely our boy."

The soup momentarily halted the conversation, and then Geek chimed in. "We should also try to get GPS surveillance on the vehicle as well as a loose tail. We have no clue as to what his plans are, so we should make some inquires with our usual suspects. Ricky's network is large, from here to Atlantic City, and he has contacts all over the place. Maybe it was a contract, maybe not, but we need to turn up the heat on some of our connected friends."

"Nothing new on the prints, yet," Ashley Stone said. "Still early, but I'm running them through APHIS again for a lucky number-ten match. I bet I'll get it too." As she said it, a tender look passed between Davis and her. From beneath the cover of the table feet were connecting like high school kids at the dinner table. She suppressed the flush of red that threatened to tinge her cheeks.

The plan was standard police work, but someone had to have seen somebody bringing the victim to the site or at least leaving it.

"We can check the newscasts and photos. Check the workers at the site and ask the media to put out a request if there were any gawkers who noticed anything," Davis said in his methodical manner.

The check arrived at the table with the standard orange wedges and fortune cookies placed neatly on top. Davis reached into his pocket and removed two twenties, which he placed on the plastic tray. Stone simultaneously reached for the cellophane-wrapped treat. She removed the plastic and crunched the cookie between her fingers, extracting the words of wisdom. She read, "A woman who seeks to be equal with men lacks ambition."

"Ouch," Geek said. "Either you have X-ray vision or Confucius really did have a sense of humor behind all those rolls of fat."

Davis smiled and pulled a second one from the tray. He read, "A fanatic is one who can't change his mind and won't change the subject." They all laughed.

"How fitting," Stone and Geek said in unison.

Stone snatched the first cookie she could grab and obliterated it in her hands. The table laughed at her antics but listened to the prize she ended up receiving. "A secret rendezvous," she read, "is close to brightening your day."

"Ooh!" Diamond cooed. "Better pass that one to Kelley. Probably hasn't seen a rendezvous since he bought the wedding ring."

"I'll pass," Geek said as he pushed back the chair and rose to leave.

They left the restaurant and headed back to the Roundhouse. There was work to do, people to call, and a murder to solve.

CHAPTER XI

Rick spent a lazy afternoon at the pool sipping a rum umbrella drink and reading the latest Patterson bestseller, a release as regular as social security checks, on time at the beginning of every month. He let his mind wander as it had been doing since his arrival.

His mind focused on Carl. He again wondered why Carl had betrayed him and if he would have done the same thing in Carl's shoes. *I don't think so,* he mused. Unlike Carl, Rick was more of a stand-up guy who would never give up a close friend. They had top lawyers and some particular influence with their multiple connections. Neither had served any serious time in the past, and the latest bust could have been *fixed* or pled down to a lesser offence. Rick was also a survivor and would do whatever it took in the name of self-preservation. The more he rationalized his actions, the more his guilt ebbed. He sipped his cocktail and his thoughts moved on.

He reached over to the small table and picked up a Monte Cristo #5 and pursed it between his lips. He uncovered his Zippo and tugged on the fat end of the cigar, inhaling the sweet, fresh smoke. His lips formed a circle, and he exhaled a grayish circle that floated listlessly across the horizon. He repeated the process, this time shooting a second smaller ring through the first. Even the Soviet judges would score them a 9.5, he thought.

As the peach-colored sun gently dipped into the aquamarine Caribbean Sea, his mind focused in on his current reality. He would be the prime suspect in the death of his partner, no ifs, ands, or buts. He was confident his alibi was as solid and protected as the gold in Fort Knox. First there was the poker game and then the girl he'd paid off.

He had made her practice her story, location, and timelines. The five large ones in cash had sealed the deal. And she was an old loyal friend. *Nothing can go wrong,* he thought and convinced himself that nothing would. Their business and personal lives went way back, and she was indebted for all the business he had sent her way over the years. And besides, she was fucking great in the sack and his most requested girl.

Rick still had about an hour before his meeting with Claude at a new restaurant. Truth be told, there was a new restaurant every week on the island, depending on which way the culinary wind blew. While finishing his cigar, he gave some thought to the offer Claude had made about expanding business in the states. On one hand, he would miss some of the income that Carl had brought in. Rick had grown accustomed to a certain lifestyle, and compromise was not an option. *On the other hand, is the risk worth the reward?* He was a hustler and knew he could come up with other alternatives. He always had. He really wasn't thrilled with the idea of losing his freedom if any mistakes were made or the DEA got lucky. Risk management. His gut and common sense said not to, but he would listen to Claude and make a decision when all the facts were in.

He arose and observed the night canopy appear, filled with pulsating stars and wisps of silver clouds.

Rick grabbed his pressed Dockers off the hanger. He pulled a cotton T-shirt out of the drawer and looped the belt. He ran the brush through his hair in a north-south direction several times, grabbed his keys, wallet, and Xanax, and pulled the door shut. He was right on time, one of his personal necessities.

Rick pulled the Mustang into the dirt space in front of the address that Claude had given him. He noticed a menu hidden behind a glass cabinet in front of the entrance. Hell, he couldn't pronounce the name of the place but at least the menu was in English.

The host greeted him at the entrance and confirmed his party was waiting upstairs. He was directed to the wrought iron spiral stairs and proceeded up. The door to the room was open, and art deco lights dimly illuminated the lounge. Claude waved him over to the private outdoor area, which circled the main bar and main circular dining area. They shook hands and smiled. He noticed Esperanza was seated. Her low cut, see-through blouse readily exposed her beaming headlights. She was certainly raising his bar.

He bent over and greeted her with a kiss on the cheek. "This is so unexpected. I'm so glad you have joined us. I had no idea," he said excitedly.

"Claude said you wouldn't mind, and since we have already gotten acquainted, I am happy to see you again," she countered.

Rick knew Claude had not mentioned her joining them, perhaps to make his proposition more attractive. *She is not part of the equation,* he thought, but a good try on Claude's part. Business is best decided with a clear head.

They all took seats, with Claude and Rick sitting with their backs toward the bay in order to give Esperanza the best view. The waiter arrived, and they all ordered cocktails. They exchanged small talk, Esperanza mentioning that the chef was known for his classic French dishes and that he had cooked for many heads of state while he was in Europe. The waiter arrived and placed the drinks on the teal coasters that adorned the tables.

Claude raised his glass in a toast. "To friends, health, and wealth, and of course all the carnal pleasures associated with them," he proposed.

They all nodded and smiled, raising their glasses and sipping their agreement. Rick understood that after dinner, the business at hand would be addressed and all formalities would subside.

"May I please be excused?" Esperanza asked, her voice in a naïve seductive tone.

Both Claude and Rick stood, proving that chivalry was still alive and well. As Esperanza exited the table and turned, her napkin and lighter abruptly fell from the small cocktail table. Rick immediately bent down to retrieve the items. As his knees folded, the sound of the overhead light shattering rang out. At almost the same instance he felt a warm liquid splatter on his cheek and forehead. As he looked up, Claude was bearing down on him, half of his face missing and parts of his skull exposed. With no time to think or react, Rick's body was covered by Claude's full weight. He covered his head with his arms as he heard shrill screams erupting from all sections of the restaurant. He didn't move. He waited and listened for more destructive blasts but none followed. No sounds or movements emanated as time abruptly halted. Everything had happened so suddenly, and he had not had time to process the events.

With his head still pressed against the floor, his eyes scanned the room to see if the assailant was close by. There was no movement, and the only sounds were sobbing and heavy breathing that filled the room. His eyes gravitated in the direction in which Esperanza had exited, but he saw nothing. She wasn't on the floor, and the only casualty at this point seemed to be his host.

His mind started racing, trying to evaluate the series of events that had just occurred. *Did Esperanza make it out or was she the target? Was she the mastermind? Was I the target? Or only Claude? Or all three?* One thing was certain: Claude was dead. Esperanza was probably long gone.

In the faint distance the sounds of high-pitched sirens emerged. As they neared, crimson and blue lights started to fill the darkness through the open porch.

"Is anyone hurt?" came a shaky voice from the room.

"A man is, down here. He's been shot, and I believe he's dead," Rick answered in a steady voice.

"Help is almost here. Stay calm. This will all be sorted out."

The sound of running footsteps materialized as someone barked orders to what seemed like an army. The footsteps dispersed in numerous directions, one being the iron stairway. As someone arrived at the landing the voice told everyone to stay calm and remain where they were. It was going to be a long evening.

The lights appeared as the hum of a generator filled the room. Patrons slowly began to right themselves and take their seats at their tables. Sporadic lights flashed as customers lit up cigarettes to calm their nerves. Drinks were gulped, not sipped.

A baritone voice filled the open room. "Ladies and gentlemen, the premises are now secure, and you may all relax. Please return to where you were as this unfortunate incident occurred. My men will be visiting you, asking some questions, so please be cooperative."

There were roughly fifteen people in the room, including customers and staff. They all shuffled to their designated spots. Two policemen were straddled over Claude's body, talking in low whispers and sharing information. Even Stevie Wonder could have seen that the wound was inflicted by a high-velocity hollow point that had shattered upon impact. There had been no audible gunshot sounds within even close proximity to the room. The shot had to have come from several hundred yards away with some type of assault weapon. And this event had been carried out by a very accurate sniper.

The EMTs entered, wheeling the mandatory gurney that held a black neoprene rubber bag on its platform. The area was then cordoned off with a bright roll of red tape that read

Hurricane Damaged Area—Please Avoid

in dark bold letters. One must assume murder is not a common occurrence in paradise, so the yellow CSI tape was not in inventory.

Several hours later, the police cleared the room. All necessary photos were snapped and the lone investigator was brushing off the last fingerprint dust. Rick suddenly recalled that Esperanza was absent, and he wondered if he should make this fact known to the authorities.

No way, he mused. He still was clueless about any of the current events that had just unfolded. Silence would be golden, and he would not get involved. As he exited onto the street, crowds were beginning to disperse. The show was over and his vacation was coming to an abrupt halt.

Rick pulled open the door of his Mustang and crawled into the weekend traffic to Lee's. He was famished, and a burger and fries would satiate his appetite as well as relax his nerves.

He took a stool at the bar and faced the street. He was cautious and felt some minor paranoia setting in. He had a shot of brandy and a Heineken as he awaited his meal. He knew what he must do. The airport opened at eight, so he would drop off the car and search for the first flight back to the states. He didn't think he would be safe to remain on the island and had no idea if he was a hunted man. It dawned on him that his business on the island was now shut down permanently, which, along with his lost revenue in Carl, would mean a new money-making venture was in order. He would talk to his connections and worry about that later.

His dinner came along with a second round of drinks. He knew there would be connecting flights to Miami, San Juan, and Charlotte the next day. There were also direct flights to New York and Philadelphia, so the odds were in his favor that his exit would be probable.

He finished his burger and waited until the 1:00 a.m. closing before he took off. He was in no rush to return to the timeshare, just in case it was under surveillance. He drove to the nearby casino in Maho Bay, heading to the rear of the floor so he could observe the comings and goings. He would remain awake till the sun came up and then return, pack, and head to the airport.

Chapter XII

As the sun set in the City of Brotherly Love 1675 miles north of Ricky Grosse, Davis returned to his two-bedroom townhouse. He tossed his coat down, threw the stack of manila folders on his kitchen work table, and grabbed a beer. It was Friday night, and no plans were imminent, other than his obsession with the case. Tomorrow he would make his customary bimonthly trip to see his brother, a computer whiz commonly called on for high-profile cases by various government departments. Maybe Davis would take the case with him for a fresh point-of-view. It couldn't hurt.

He flipped the switch, and florescent bulbs illuminated the dark kitchen. He pulled over the file marked **SURVEILLANCE** and opened it. The first page had Rick's plane reservations and itinerary. He noted the return flight was scheduled for Sunday, but the airlines and Homeland Security would alert him if plans changed. He noticed it was his eighth trip to St. Maarten within the past three years. No way these were all pleasure trips. He'd meant to circle the dates in red, but Ellen Sue already did. He smiled. Got to love efficiency.

So far one of the biggest parts of the case, the bombing, was nothing to be excited over. Other than its complete efficiency of scattering Davis's crime scene over a couple stories worth of rubble, it did little else to assist his case. The building needed demolishing. It was blown up. Case closed.

Davis reached for his beer and noticed the moisture running down the bottle. He was so immersed in his reading that the beer had reached room temperature, and its mountains were no longer blue. Now it was simply undrinkable. He pushed his chair away from the table and carried his beer to the sink, spilling it down the drain. As he opened the fridge to grab another, he noticed that almost two hours had passed. His stomach let him know it was feeding time.

At that instant, a knocking came from his front door. He wasn't expecting any company, but he needed a slight break.

"State your name," he only half jokingly called out.

"Dinner, Mr. Davis," bellowed an unmistakable female voice. "And a murder!"

"Be right there, Ms. Stone," he replied, recognizing Ashley's voice.

He turned the deadbolt and immediately opened the door. A white pizza box with the familiar *You've tried the rest, now try the Best!* logo was thrust into his hands. She pushed her way past him carrying a white bag along with a crumpled brown bag containing what appeared to be the accompanying wine or the tallest bag of onion rings ever.

"No need to invite me in, I'm in already," she said with a laugh. She noticed that the table was completely covered in folders, legal pads, sharpies, photos, and some blank search warrants.

"I didn't realize Katrina made it this far north," she chided. "Time to clean off the table so we can at least experience some normalcy."

Davis obliged, making neat stacks to not disturb the order of his priorities. Ashley laid the box on the table. She opened it as a magician would, slowly revealing a thin-crust pizza, half steak and half eggplant.

She knew it was his favorite. As she removed the appetizer portion of fried calamari—a peculiar staple of a Philadelphian pizzeria—she glanced over at him and detected a smile.

"Now go retrieve two wine glasses while I freshen up," she ordered.

"Is there anything else, your highness?" he asked, but she was already in his bathroom.

She emerged from his room, her cheeks a little rosier and eyeliner slightly darker. He pulled the chair out for her and then sat beside her. She covered the paper plate with a slice of each side of pizza as he handed her a fork and napkin. They began with the pizza, discussing some aspects of the case. He outlined where he was and what he still needed to finish. He told her they would meet Grosse at the airport and escort him to their *house* downtown. They would also be speaking to several other persons of interest, those who were recipients of his Wednesday night calls. They sipped their Merlot and smiled. When they were done, Ashley removed the paper plates and empty box, placing them in the disposal. The leftover pizza found a place in the fridge next to several other containers filled with leftovers.

As she returned to the table, she stopped behind him. She leaned down and kissed the back of his neck with her moist lips. At the same time, she slid her hands down the front of his shirt, her fingers simultaneously pinching his nipples hard enough to evoke a response of both pleasure and pain. As his breathing grew heavier, he went to stand up, but she pushed his shoulders down so she could excite him further. When he finally arose, he turned to face her. He grabbed her buttocks and lifted her off the floor. She was surprised, and to retaliate she lifted her legs parallel to the floor and wrapped them around him.

He carried her to the overstuffed couch and dropped her, watching her unexpected reaction. As she laughed, he slid down, knees on the hardwood floor, and pushed her legs outward. Knowing what to expect, she groped to remove her blouse with one arm and unbuttoned her jeans with the other. As she did, he pulled the zipper down and tugged while she wriggled her jeans free. His right hand lowered her panties, and she lifted her ass in anticipation. His head nuzzled between her thighs. He pushed her legs further apart as his tongue lightly touched her favorite place. It wiggled north and south at first and then moved in circles. As his speed and intensity increased, hers did as well. Within seconds she let out a scream as she exploded all over his face. Total ecstasy consumed her.

Filled with passion and a sensory overload, Ashley ordered him to lay face up on the couch. He gladly complied. She then straddled his hips and slid him inside her. As she lifted her body and slid down, her knee slipped between the seat cushions. They laughed in unison. Knowing the saying about getting thrown off the horse, she quickly remounted her steed and finished the job she had started. This interlude lasted longer than the quickies they sneaked in during office hours. Longer than their office rousts, they termed this act a "meddi" since it was somewhere in the middle of a quickie and the all-nighter longy, Davis felt the word was appropriate.

As she dismounted she sat on the couch and lifted his legs on to her lap.

"Will you be joining me for breakfast?" he asked in a playful tone.

"As long as you're driving, I'm in."

"Good. We can set the alarm for eight. Now let's go to the boudoir, my queen, so you can show me act two."

The apartment went dark.

CHAPTER XIII

At seven in the morning, Davis's cell phone went off. He pulled the cell out of the charger and said, "This better be good."

"It's Jake Jeffe here, Davis. I have some developments on your rabbit."

Jake was his contact at Homeland Security, who was currently monitoring Grosse's movements abroad. "It seems he has changed his vacation plans a tad. He'll be catching the 8:10 a.m. flight out of St. Maartin. There's a layover in Chicago. I'll put a man at the airport just in case he misses the connection to Philly."

"What's his ETA, Jake?"

"It touches down at 4:47 a.m., gate E."

"I owe ya one, thanks."

Ashley felt a cold hand run down her neck. She was startled and jerked herself up. She opened her eyes and lazily asked, "Who was that?"

"It was Jeffe over at Homeland. Grosse is on the move. He caught an early flight out of St. Maartin and is heading back here with a stopover in Chicago," Davis explained. "We need to pick it up. Let's get the breakfast I promised, pick up that search warrant, and get to the airport. I'll call my brother, tell him I'm postponing our tea party."

With their game faces on, they each began to prepare for the long day.

"You shower first," Davis called. "I'm going to make some arrangements so we can meet over at Grosse's apartment around 11:00."

Twenty-odd minutes later, they were dressed and out the front door.

"You drive," he barked, tossing her the keys to the Bronco.

"Where to?" she asked.

"I like the Oregon Diner. Best home fries in the city."

They finished breakfast, and Davis paid the waitress. They left the diner and jumped into the Bronco. They headed back up Broad toward Locust. A quick phone call at breakfast told them the warrant was now in hand. The scene was in the opposite direction, making it necessary for them to drive past Davis's place. They decided to pick up Ashley's car along the way so she could meet him on-scene. They at least had to keep appearances up.

Five of the nine Organized Crime Task Force members stood outside the apartment as Geek approached, warrant in hand, signed the night before by Judge Chambers.

"Gather 'round, troops," Geek said. "Let me read this warrant so we are all on the same page. We are authorized to search and seize the following items pursuant to this case, yada yada. They are as follows: any and all weapons, ammunition, or permits for the previous mentioned items. Any syringes, pharmaceutical labeled vials, or illicit narcotics. Make sure all prescriptions in the bathroom have Mr. Grosse's names on them. All computers, hard drives, banking materials, and checkbooks will be confiscated. Any date books, diaries, and materials that relate to *Full Service Concierges* may also be seized. Let's play this one close to the chest so nothing gets thrown out on a technicality."

They all knew procedure. They separated into groups of two and entered the residence. It was a little past noon, and time was not a factor. Ashley and Davis teamed up and headed for the bathroom. Inside the medicine cabinet were the standard containers of daily health and beauty items. They were greatly outnumbered by a large clutter of prescription bottles.

"Looks like he has the same doctor Elvis had," Ashley joked. The bad news was that they were all legal and up-to-date. There were no syringes or indictable containers.

In the office, Geek and Ellen Sue went through several file cabinets and their contents. They slid several that looked useful into a plastic bag. Geek pulled out a small leather case that looked like a burglary kit but was in actuality filled with tools for dissecting a computer. Rather than hassle, he unplugged the tower and placed it in an evidence box, labeling its contents.

The last team went through bedrooms items, pulling out drawers and sliding hangers aside in the closet. After several hours had passed, the team was slightly disappointed with their take. Several notebooks, a computer, and some downloaded bank statements were all they could confiscate. It would be hours until they could learn if any useful information was now in their possession. Davis hoped something might be gathered prior to the upcoming interview with their main person of interest.

Occasionally during a search warrant it is the officer's intent to let their presence go unknown, at least temporarily on the premises. All furniture is rearranged, the desks are reorganized, and even refrigerator contents replaced to keep the subject from knowing that their home has been invaded at least temporarily. This was not the case for the OCTF. By clean up time, most of the team had left without bothering. The more pissed off the suspect was over the intrusion, the more likely his emotions would trump his caution and logic.

The connection in Chicago was on time, which was not all that common. Rick listened to his i-Pod and thumbed through the plane's *Sky Mall* magazine, a catalog filled with overpriced, status-filled items that were at the same time entertaining. Rick chuckled at the useless merchandise. A mini remote control helicopter was the cover feature.

The plane touched down and headed for gate E18 at the overseas terminal. That meant a half-mile walk through mazes, down escalators, and through customs. He wasn't concerned about the box of Cubans he was bringing back for his clientele.

He touched his i-Phone and connected to the straggling voice mails and e-mails that had never crossed the Atlantic or cyberspace. The first voice mail was from his favorite female alibi, Abbey, informing him the police were coming by on Sunday and that she was straight on their story. She also mentioned that Carl's body had been released and the funeral would be held up in the Northeast on Sunday. The second was from a client who wanted a meeting and needed some work. He would talk at the funeral. He erased all incoming messages and arrived at the yellow line in customs.

He easily checked through, answering the obligatory questions about illegal contraband, money, fruits, and vegetables. The agent lowered her screen, checked for any outstanding warrants or alerts, and then smiled and let him pass.

He waited in a large room filled with luggage carousels and preceded to #3, where his bags would arrive. A muffled foghorn was followed by a yellow flashing light and the carousel started its clockwise rotation. Several minutes later he spotted his olive Cardin Pullman and approached it. He jerked it off and released the handle. He followed the line leading to the final inspection and waited. He handed the agent his immigration card, was given a cursory glance, and was then waived through. He pulled out his phone to call for a car when he felt two arms on his shoulder, halting his momentum.

"Welcome home, Ricky," Davis stated. "I hope you had a wonderful vacation."

"Until now, Davis. And the name's Rick, not Ricky. To what do I owe this pleasure? Are you offering me a ride home?" he sarcastically said. He looked at the other agent, noting the guy was Gerald Eckland, one of Davis's "core of four."

"Yes and no," Davis replied. "We did come to pick you up, but before you get home, I thought you'd stop by our house for a short chat. Much has happened since your little trip."

"Is this official? Should I call my attorney?"

"Why would you think you'd need an attorney? Let's just say it's a strong request. It shouldn't take more than an hour or so."

With those pleasantries exchanged, they left the terminal and got into Davis's Bronco, Geek in front and Grosse in the back.

Chapter XIV

The trio entered the building through the rear entrance closest to where they had parked. They rode the elevator up to the fourth floor, took a right, and headed for a room marked Interview 3.

The room had two chairs facing a third, which was pushed back into the far corner of the room. It was eggshell white, the smell of newly applied paint still lingering. The brass thought the room had looked stereotypically like a set from *Law and Order,* so the cafeteria green was laid to rest.

Davis pointed to the chair in the back and asked Rick to please sit. Rick walked over to the chair, lifted it, and put it in the middle of the room.

"Cut the crap, guys." Rick snorted. "I really don't want to feel hemmed in by you two. As you said earlier, it's not official."

Davis led off, expressing condolences for Carl. He told Rick how they had found him and where, watching for any reactions that might be a tell. Rick sat stoically, with no emotions coming. He was a poker player too.

"It's a shame," Rick replied. "Carl and I went way back. We shared many things together for quite a long time. I was crushed when I learned of his accident late Thursday. It was no way to start a vacation."

"You were so upset that you hopped the next flight back, I see."

"Was nothing I could have done. I needed the time away, and besides, Carl would have done the same thing."

"The autopsy puts the time of death sometime around the evening before you left. We're going to need to know where you were. You understand," Davis goaded.

"You know damn well where I was or you wouldn't have asked me that question," Rick curtly replied. "I was with Abbey Road, who you may know as Jessica Rand. We hooked up and spent the night together. Before that I was winning a poker game—or losing, with all the money I left there."

They had assumed this; her number was the last number to appear on his cell records that evening. Rick was correct, as they had already set up an appointment to talk with her tomorrow. They knew she was an escort at *Philly Phlesh*, an upscale whorehouse that Rick was said to be a silent partner in. His poker buddies had already been interviewed, and Rick's alibi was air tight. However, it was the time after he left to see Ms. Abbey Road that the team really wanted.

Geek jumped in. "We have you computer and are going through the hard drive. Should we expect any revelations you may be keeping from us?"

"Knock yourselves out, guys," Rick said with a confident, macho arrogance.

He flat out annoyed them. It would be time before others were questioned and the whole picture would develop. One of the goals of this exercise was to put Rick on notice that he was their primary person of interest. He had the means and an unquestionable motive, but they had to break his hidden opportunity. And they would be the ones to break it.

Davis and Eckland had attended several courses at the FBI's Behavioral Science Unit at Quantico. They excelled at their studies and on many occasions had used what they'd learned. They took away several key points. A favorite was to always keep the subject off guard by not following timelines and shooting random questions at him.

Also important was to observe body language for certain improprieties, such as when eyes looked down and to the left because deception usually followed. Folding one's arms could mean the subject was hiding something and that you were on the right track. They also liked to repeat questions in the hope of receiving contradictory answers. There were many more tactics, but these were their bread and butter.

They started by showing a picture of Carl's remains, trying to gauge a reaction, but there was none. They asked about several of his connections in the city, but his answers were mundane. He was experienced in the art of interrogation too, but from the criminal end. He learned not to express emotion or voluntarily give up information. He asked no questions and gave no replies. End of story.

They pressed on, letting him know some of the things Carl had told them, but they left the sources unnamed. They correctly named some of his clients and activities, also mentioning they were following these leads. No matter what they brought up, they still didn't have enough for an arrest. Rick would have to exercise more caution and planning if he were to continue his illicit activities. They concluded the interview by asking him to stay available and not leave town without checking in.

He'd expected a more intense volley of accusations, but they never came. It was game time and the clock had begun. As Rick rose, he handed them his lawyer's card, his way of saying to contact him if any further questions arose. It was late and he was tired.

"If there are no further questions, I'm going to call my car service for a ride."

"Not at this time," both of his interrogators answered in near unison.

Rick left.

They decided to call it a night. It had been a long day, and tomorrow the OCTF team would attend the funeral from afar—but not until all surveillance devices were in place.

CHAPTER XV

The next morning Jim Kelley and Geek met early at the Wawa down on Frankford Avenue.

They left with two twenty-four-ounce French Roasts and proceeded to the church where the service would take place. They found neighboring apartment sanctioned for the stakeout, entered, and carried some equipment to the roof. One of their favorites was a Parabolic brand listening device that could hear sounds up to three hundred feet away. Kelley wondered aloud if every NFL team owns one. Geek pointed out they were probably as illegal as lip readers.

The two set up a video recorder below so that video would accompany the voices. They next plotted the area where pictures could be snapped with a good line of visibility that was not too obvious. It was ten o' clock, and they had time to spare.

Davis and Ellen Sue Diamond were motoring downtown for an appointment with Abbey Road. They needed to see if they believed her story, which corroborated Rick's alibi. They needed to pin down a timeline, any witnesses, and anything else they could use to refute Rick's story. They pulled up to her Center City Townhouse and slipped a card that read **POLICE BUSINESS** beneath the wiper.

They left the car and walked up the two steps. They used the brass knocker that hung on a solid red door, knocking twice.

About a minute later, a woman's throaty voice replied. "If you don't call, I don't know who you are, so if you have my number, use it."

"We're looking for Ms. Rand or Ms. Road, not sure what you go by this morning," Davis replied. "We did have an appointment. We're investigating a homicide and we *did* call."

"Hold your creds up to the door so I can see them," she answered. After deciding they looked legit, she removed the chain and opened the door. "Call me Abbey Road. It's kinda grown on me, and I do like the Beatles. And with whom will I be speaking to?"

"Mr. Mustard and Polythene Pam," Davis said comically.

"Gee, that's a new one," she replied, total sarcasm etched in her voice.

"Sorry," Davis said. "I just had to."

They entered the small, well appointed sitting room. She actually did like the Beatles. They noticed some framed album covers and a couple of posters from the early years before Sgt. Pepper. The room was a combination of art deco and pre-Woodstock.

She offered them a seat in the living room and asked if they wanted a drink. Ellen asked for a coffee and Davis requested water. She headed into the kitchenette and returned with the water and mentioned the coffee would be a minute. She turned to the bar and poured herself a clear liquid out of a Ketel One bottle.

She sat down across from them and sighed. "Fire away," she said.

"First, we are not with vice and don't really care about how you earn a living." Ellen removed a picture from her folder and at the same time asked if Abbey had known Carl Mickels.

She glanced at the picture and replied, "He was one of Rick's friends, but we only met a few times."

"He was found buried under the parking garage they were demolishing near the zoo, as you may have read. It was a homicide, and that's why we're here."

Abbey shrugged nonchalantly.

"We need to verify Rick's alibi. He said you two spent the Wednesday night Carl was killed together, and we'd like your account."

"Let's see. I drove over to his place on Locust. I had to park behind the building, so I used the service entrance, which is always open. I got there about 8:00 or 8:30 p.m. We chatted, had some drinks, and crawled into bed. That's the story," she said.

Davis had his spiral notebook open and was selectively writing things down. He would see if this jibed with Rick's account during the next interview. Abbey seemed very matter-of-fact and was not volunteering anything extra. That alone seemed familiar, and any story too rehearsed was probably a fake.

"How long have you known him?" Ellen queried.

"About ten or twelve years," she replied. "He was referred to me, we hit it off, and the rest is history, as they say." Abbey sipped her drink and then told Ellen she would be right back with her coffee.

When she returned, Davis said, "Abbey, if you're withholding anything from us, you'll be charged as an accessory. You'll be treated as any other suspect and your life will—how shall I say it …?—*suck*. If you're lying for him or protecting him, we will find out. We're good at what we do and have the best rate of solving cases. Do you follow me?"

Abbey sat still and said nothing. They had no evidence, and she was tough. She would stick by her story and ignore their threats.

"I understand totally," she whispered. "Now unless I'm to be charged with anything, please leave my residence. If I must I will call my attorney, and I have a funeral to attend. Good day!"

During the questioning, Ellen had a puzzled look on her face. David was deviating from his normal barrage of hard-hitting questions, usually fired with no mercy. But now he was much calmer and passive. He must have had a good reason. Everything he did had a reason and his percentage of solving cases *was* off the charts.

Davis did not leave at first. Instead, he asked several more questions in regard to her history with both Carl and Rick. All of her answers were slow and deliberate, indicating that she didn't want to stray from some rehearsed script and continued to not voluntarily give up a thing.

Ellen Sue and Davis stood up to leave.

Davis's tone and mood took a 180-degree turn. "Think good and hard about this, Abbey. We can and will be pricks if need be. You will go down if you're covering anything up. Thanks for the drinks and have a nice day," he said, his voice lowered as he concluded.

They turned and without a word left the house. The door shut firmly behind them, indicating they had upset her a bit. This was good. They smiled at each other, knowing they had at least accomplished something.

As they entered the car, Davis held up his hand in anticipation of Ellen's question. "Let me explain what just happened. We're dealing with two street smart individuals here. Do I believe they're involved? Hell, yeah. Her body language screams cover up. Rick did this crime. You know it and so does the rest of the team. She's his alibi and she will now think long and hard if she wants to go the distance for him, if it's a lie. If she did spend the night with him, it's possible she's more involved than she appears. Do you think she might have lured Carl somewhere? Eventually leading to his demise?"

She was lost in all the possibilities he had presented and was thinking aloud. "Not sure. Maybe Rick stepped out while they were hooking up. Maybe he drugged her. Her timeframe is off."

"That's why we're detectives," he joked.

"My gut says she's not that daring to help with the murder. I have to go with the alibi angle. It's possible she owed him something. Maybe he raised her stake in the club? Paid her off? Threatened her? Whatever the reason, we should question the doorman at Rick's building and get a hold of the video surveillance tapes. I'll get on it after the funeral," she said.

"By the way," Davis said. "Carl had a small insurance policy, a couple hundred thousand, but he left it to various kid charities. Carl grew up as kind of a loner and spent a year in protective services when his father split. His mom had a major breakdown and there was no family to speak of. His mom eventually got it together and was granted custody. She followed all the guidelines and kept him in line until his eighteenth birthday."

"You kind of liked Carl, I see," she said. This level of detail wasn't unheard of in Davis, but it was rare.

"I didn't know him that well. He had only started cooperating six or so weeks ago. He gave the impression of his interest in a life of crime as well as becoming a little fearful of Rick. He also realized he couldn't risk getting arrested again at this stage in life. He was trying to reform. He did give us enough information to start some investigations, and if we don't nail Rick, it's moot."

As they turned on to Frankford, Ellen requested he stop at the next corner. They pulled over, and Ellen got out and vanished into Wawa. After several minutes she came out, smiling. Davis leaned over and swung open her door, and she got in.

"Chivalry is alive and well in Philadelphia," she teased.

"And so it is," he parried.

She pulled two objects out of the plastic bag and handed him a Klondike Bar. She grabbed the wooden stick and produced a Cherry Garcia bar, which she hurriedly unwrapped.

"Cheers," she exclaimed, clinking the bars together and devouring a big bite.

The church was still several blocks away when Ellen Sue's phone rang. She answered, and Kelley told them to meet up on the rooftop surveillance of the white building numbered 364. It was far enough away from the arena they were studying that they would not be recognized by some of the mourners whom they may have arrested in the past. Between the hyperbolic mike and the telephoto video recorder and monitor, they could watch the whole service as if from their living room.

Davis and Ellen took the rear service elevator and rode up to the rooftop. The ledge held the cameras, hidden amid satellite dishes and security cameras. They leaned against the door, Geek holding a device that could freeze frames and snap photos. With another button they could be e-mailed directly to headquarters and be given a name and current address.

Davis's mind wandered back to Ellen's ring tone ("Shining Star" by Earth, Wind, and Fire). When she attended Yale, she was called the shining star by much of the faculty. She had almost finished her dual degree in criminal justice and statistics. She was fascinated by the possibility of linking the two in computer programs to predict criminal behavior and patterns. The unfortunate part was that her obsession with statistics had led her to Mohegan Sun, the Indian Casino fifty miles away. Blackjack was her main statistics project, and she was a fast learner. One night she won more than $17,000 and left before the card cycles changed. Although cards are random, they can "turn on you" and beat you as badly as you have beaten the house. She left the cashier's cage and headed for a closed outdoor lot. Security escorted her out, his hand clutching his holstered sidearm. She thanked him and headed toward I-95 and New Haven.

Several miles later at a light near an entrance ramp, a car struck hers with a metal on metal *thunk*. Both drivers got out, but in the moonless night she could not see the stocking covering his face or the hunting knife at his side. As they neared, he pressed the serrated edges of the knife across her windpipe and grabbed her purse. He pushed her down, slammed the butt of the knife against her head, and rolled her into a shallow ravine at the roadside.

After a difficult recovery, she graduated with honors. She was still a shining star and would use her brains to hunt down other criminals, which gave her a sense of getting even.

As the courtyard filled up, shutters were clicking and the tape was rolling. They noticed some of Carl's customers, such as Ben Kaplan, a high roller from New York who owned several very successful restaurant franchises. Carl would hook him up with women and sports tickets whenever the Giants or Mets were in town.

Also in attendance were several low-level mob guys who worked for splinter groups. When Merlino and Stanfa went on hiatus, the Philadelphia mob had no unifying leader to speak of. Smaller groups carved their own turf and services, with a surprisingly low level of violence perpetrated on the citizens of the city of Brotherly Love. The philosophy was there was enough business to go around, and greed wasn't as good as Michael Douglas led you to believe in *Wall Street*. It worked with minimal problems.

The problems of Jamaican, Russian, and Asian gangs were becoming a far more complicated issue. The Organized Crime Task Force was underfunded, understaffed, and overworked, which made the job even tougher.

Through his night-vision goggles Davis saw a familiar face, that of Julian Gando, a man with a reputation. Julian was sort of liaison, a go between, linking some of the New York families with Philadelphia groups. He was rumored to have committed several hits on those who were getting too cocky or greedy. According to his file, he was also rumored to oversee conflicts and partnerships with certain business that linked the two cities. This would keep or at least limit the infringement from other ethnic criminal competitors. In essence, the small timers stayed small and the bigger rivals suddenly disappeared over a bridge, found themselves strapped to a booby-trapped car, or were shot in crowded bars. With all these rumors, nothing was ever proved nor was Gando ever arrested.

Gando made his way over to Rick. He gave him a sympathetic hug and whispered, "I'm very sorry for your loss. Carl was a good man. There might be some cops here so I don't want to talk. I need you to get in touch."

Rick felt his suit pocket separate and a piece of paper fall into the lining. Julian patted his back again and separated. Rick had done work for Julian in the past relaying messages, making threats, and getting some inside information. Each time the job had been completed to Julian's satisfaction. Rick knew some of his income would be vanishing due to events that had occurred over the past several days. He would welcome some work. He would read the note in the privacy of his own home. He was a cautious man.

Several more familiar faces dotted the crowd, but none were as big a fish as Gando. When they got back to the station they would check warrants with the pictures they had taken and see if any more suspects emerged. It was only day four of the investigation, well past the critical first forty-eight hours, a benchmark timeframe for making an arrest before things went cold.

As the end of the eulogy approached, they watched the screen. Mentions were made of Carl's positive contributions in life and to that of his community and church. They spoke of his devotion to God and his fellow man. There was no mention of his misdeeds or errant ways that had led to criminal activities. He sure wasn't a saint, and bookmakers jokingly gave 6–5 odds he wouldn't be making a trip "up north" after the burial.

Geek picked up his cell and punched in Jimmy Kelley's number and asked him to come up to the roof and help pack up the equipment. He was the rookie to the squad, the gopher, and he would have to get used to taking orders—he was getting married soon. He arrived moments later and helped them finish up. They lugged the high tech equipment over to the service elevator and would go back to the Roundhouse for what promised to be a fifteen-minute debriefing by Davis. He was always punctual, and fifteen minutes never meant sixteen.

Rick was shaking hands and playing host as the rest of the mourners left the short service. His hand felt the note Gando had slipped inside his pocket. He was anxious to read it. When the crowd dispersed, he headed down the street to get his car, occasionally glancing over his shoulders to see if he was being followed. He took a small black box out of his inside pocket and walked around his car, holding the box at hip level. The box was the size of a deck of cards and had a green and red light. As long as the green indicator light remained on, there were no indications that any electronic tracking equipment had been placed on his vehicle. He was a *careful* man. He got in, started the car, and headed to the sanctity of a dinner at Capital Grille.

Three blocks down the street, the team entered their vehicles and headed back to the office. Their dinners would come out of vending machines. It would be peanuts and cheese crackers for now, not a twenty-ounce steak and onion rings, which their prey would probably be dining on. They arrived and quickly convened in the conference room as Davis began to summarize.

"I want to thank you all for putting in the extra time on this investigation. I don't have to tell you how badly I want to solve this case. We gathered a lot more pictures and information tonight. We can sort out the pictures and tapes and will reformulate our next steps as soon as we have organized this information.

"On Monday I'll give you your assignments and we'll begin squeezing some of these lowlifes. I'm confident we can close this investigation in the coming weeks. As far as the means to commit this crime, we might as well open the Philadelphia phone book and pick a name. Motive will be more specific. It might have been revenge, or maybe a past debt that Carl screwed someone over with. God help us if was some psychopath, gang initiation, or spree killing we have no clue about. And as far as the opportunity, we'll focus on his cell phone list and those we saw today at the funeral. I'd like to thank all of you for the time and dedication you are showing on this case. You are all a great bunch of professionals, and your dedication is awesome. Now get out of here and take the rest of the weekend off."

It was Sunday night. The weekend was over.

"Thanks, boss," Ashley said sarcastically. "I'll make sure the last ten hours of this weekend are the best of my life."

The room emptied, and everyone left for the night.

Rick entered the bar at the Capital Grille and gave a sign to the bartender for his usual double brandy. He gazed around at the bar area before he removed the note from his pocket. He opened it and read it. The message was short: "W8Ralphs." It was not a sophisticated code but the way he and Julian communicated. It simply meant dinner at Ralph's in South Philly on Wednesday night at eight o'clock. There was no need to confirm as he would be expected to attend, barring any natural disasters. He had no clue as to what the meeting was about, but it surely meant there was a job to do and the pay would be generous.

Rick ate dinner and skipped desert. It had been a long five days and there would be work to do and people to see in the coming week.

PART TWO

Chapter XVI

It was a beautiful May morning when Rick woke, a good day to start his "new reality," as he phrased it. He was not being stalked by the cops, and his interest was piqued for his meeting with Julian Gando. He had a shopping list of things to accomplish before Wednesday. First on his list was to send Abbey a small thank you for her nerve and cooperation with his alibi. She hadn't budged from her story. He promptly dialed the local flower shop and ordered an assortment of colorful roses, tulips, and some exotic-looking crossbreeds. The entire note would read "You are awesome." He then made some calls to his clients, mentioning he was back in town and that some of his services would be on hold. He left them his disposable cell phone number, mentioning only to call in case of an emergency. He would be back up on Thursday.

At seven in the morning Davis arrived at the Roundhouse. He headed up to the fourth floor, anxious to see if any new reports had come in. A small stack of folders sat his desk. He grabbed a drink and sat down to examine them.

The first contained the forensics reports from the crime scene. Because the scene had been so compromised by the rubble and latter excavation, it was of no use. No DNA evidence had been found on the shell casings or the plastic ties that surrounded Carl's wrists. The next folder contained various bank records from Carl and Rick. Their joint account contained several thousand dollars, but that was a reasonable amount. A list of the past month's checks were listed. They included car services, restaurants, rent for their offices, and the cleaning service. Nothing out of the ordinary jumped off the page. Davis needed to find some type of transaction that was unrelated to their daily expenditures. He needed names, something he could tie to a payoff, bribe, or hush money. Nothing he examined fit that scenario. He knew Rick was smart, cunning, and deliberate in what he did. It would not be easy, but the case *would* be solved. After all, it was written in his notebook, and everything written there came to an end.

Rick was psyched. He had tickets for the businessmen's special at the ballpark. The Phillies were playing the Reds and Halliday was pitching. He even threw two grand down on the game with the hope of winning twelve hundred more. He loved the action. He called Artie Klugmeyer, his game day buddy, and said he would stop at Genos and bring the cheese steaks "wit," meaning fully loaded "wit" the works. He told Artie to get the peanuts and a pint of brandy. What other way was there to watch an afternoon game?

Rick was getting pretty buzzed as the game entered the bottom of the seventh. Over the next two innings, the Phillies provided heart attack antics but hung on to win.

Downtown, the team was busy working on several cases. There'd been a shooting at a nearby bodega, which had been rumored to be a meth way-station run by an outlaw biker gang. Needless to say, there were no witnesses. This was a case that would remain open. The bottom line was there would be two fewer scum bags on the streets of Philadelphia.

The other involved a stock scam. It was a boiler room operation inflating the price of a bogus company that was said to have a product that would add five miles per gallon to a car's performance by attaching a device that would conserve fuel. The stock opened at five cents. It rocketed to three and a half dollars before the product was featured on Channel 6, stating that it was a fraud. All the team had to do was find out who was involved and follow the paper trail. In tough economic times, crime paid. The murder of Carl Mickels was going cold amid all the new paperwork burying it down.

Work at the Roundhouse was pretty uneventful as the team attended to its open cases. There were no new leads on Carl's recent murder, and the team was plodding through several new work loads. It would be another day for the bad guys. For now at least. But there was one good thing about justice: it had a way of taking a hunk out of a killer's hide several years post-crime. Davis didn't have that kind of patience, and neither did the rest of the task force.

But tonight was not the night to stay at his desk and ponder over his notebook. Ashley paused by his office door. She was smiling that special grin and dangling the keys to the Bronco over his face.

Tonight was definitely not the night to stay in the office. He grabbed his coat and headed out behind her.

Chapter XVII

Wednesday morning brought some light fog from the cold night air. Highs were supposed to surpass the ninety-degree mark, but the forecasters had been eleven degrees off the previous day.

Davis made his daily trip through the glass doors and up to the fourth floor. The first document on the top of his pile was from Barton Pharmaceuticals, the manufacturer and distributor of the Rocuronium Bromide that had been found in Carl's bloodstream. The letter was from the legal department, and the first sentence stated that all shipments of this product had been delivered and signed for by the facilities listed at the bottom of the report. All names that followed were area hospitals, which meant that no doctors' offices or outpatient clinics had received any product. This meant that the drug had been stolen or the person who'd injected it had had an inside contact. The hospital phone numbers would have to be checked against Rick's cell phone records, but Davis knew it would be a long shot. He would assign someone to follow it up along with the numbers on his record, which had no corresponding name.

The second correspondence was regarding a separate case that had been sent to the homicide department. It had been determined that the crime was unrelated to any organized hits and turned out to be a jilted-lover killing. Welcome to the City of Brotherly Love.

———————————

Rick was still a bit hung over from the previous day's festivities. After the game he had gone to the Capital Grille to celebrate and had overindulged. He would have to check how many people he bought drinks for, but he hoped he hadn't blown the whole twelve hundred he'd won. He picked up the remote, powered on the TV, and caught up on the day in baseball. He never got bored seeing the Phillies win but was still interested in the sport himself. Years ago, he had been paid off in pre-1960 Topps cards minus the thirty-year-old bubblegum that coated the bottom card with a white powdery substance. The gum had the dubious reputation of becoming flavorless in the first three minutes, and it took at least ten sticks to blow a major league bubble. Bazooka was the ruling bubblegum for creating air filled pockets the size of one's face.

He dabbed a few lines of his own powdery substance on the glass coffee table, rolled up a hundred dollar bill, and sniffed his day into high gear.

He flipped open his cell and left a quick message with one of his customers, a low-level detective who could check if anything new was going on in Carl's murder investigation. He knew he would be interrogated again and wanted to be prepared for it. He also needed to pick up some essentials, such as milk, bread, and coffee since he had been out of town and his fridge was empty. That would give Marci his cleaning guru time to do her thing. He slipped on his Nikes and set out for his day. The busier he remained, the less time he would have to obsess over what tonight's meeting with Gando was all about.

————————————————

Shortly after noon phones started to ring and intercoms alerted the team of an emergency in progress. Conflicting reports stated that it may or may not be an officer-involved shooting, adding another factor to their course of actions. Cooler heads do not always prevail when a fellow police officer is shot. The address came in as South Philly, the actual location being the *Goodfella Social Club*, a very well known mob hangout. It had been under electronic surveillance, which was probably why it had been called in so quickly.

Davis knew the unseasonable weather they were experiencing always incrementally increased the homicide rate. The city always appeared in the top ten of the FBI's hit list of homicides, and they were far ahead of last year's pace.

"Grab your vests and be careful out there," Davis bellowed. He and

Ellen Sue headed for the rear elevators and the Bronco while Stone and Kelley grabbed their crime scene boxes and followed closely behind. It would be a ten-minute ride with their lights and sirens, but the scene would hopefully be secured well before their arrival. Davis drove and Diamond slammed a clip into her backup Glock.

When they arrived, there was one person lying flat on the sidewalk, a pool of bright crimson liquid flowing into the crevices and down the street. Two small-caliber holes were visible in his forehead, and he was dead. The other victim was not in any better shape, having been hit once in the cheek and twice in his abdomen. His chest rose and fell in an uneven and beleaguered pattern. He was being attended to by an EMT who had been two blocks away when the call came in. The survivor was stretched out on a board and hurriedly placed on a waiting gurney. Within seconds he was deposited inside the ambulance, and they were racing to Jefferson Hospital. The speed hardly mattered. He man would be dead before he ever saw a man in a white coat.

No blue uniforms adorned the sidewalk, which was a relief to the other men in blue looking for one. Yellow crime scene tape was stretched out around several buildings up to the cars in front of the storefront. Davis barked at two of the officers to start canvassing the area for any witnesses. It would be up to Stone and Kelley to gather any items out of place and find the spent casings if a semiautomatic had been used. The crowd was herded away to give the investigators room to operate.

It was now five minutes before one o'clock and the scene was pretty secure. Davis and Diamond stood across the street talking with some of the brass. Crime was bad for a city gearing up for the summer tourists. Along with Boston, history runs through Philadelphia, and with the newer Constitution Center and Convention Center, it was attempting at making positive gains. If only the US Mint on Fifth gave away samples, it would be a destination more popular than Las Vegas.

Ashley and Kelley were about done. They needed to get some trajectory angles to pin down where the shooter had been. Bullet holes ricochets, and shell casings give a good impression, but the use of the specific poles would give them a working 3D image of the invisible trajectory lines.

"Hey, Ash," Kelley called. "Grab the extendable rods from the back of the van so we can make some guesstimates."

"Will do, partner!" she said with a giddy hop in her step.

He laughed as she switched to a wide-stance Western walk as she headed for the van parked several cars away.

Just then an ear-splitting explosion emanated from behind the large plate glass windows of the club, sending sharp glass projectiles speeding outward. In what seemed like slow motion, Kelley's face turned a blood-soaked red as the shards of glass penetrated his now limp body. A dozen milling officers turned and ran into the area from where the blast had come from with no regard of what may follow.

Kelley's face was almost unrecognizable as he writhed in excruciating pain. The roar of a deafening siren approached, as someone had had the wherewithal to call for a bus.

Davis knelt by his teammate, trying to do what he could to help while Kelley's body began to go into shock. "Give him some fucking room! Make room for the fucking bus!" Davis cried.

Tears were streaming down Ashley's eyes. It might have been her lying next to him. She wanted to run to Davis, to hold him in her arms. She wanted him to tell her it would be all right, but something kept her back. Her body shook all over.

The ambulance arrived, and the medics worked at breakneck speed to stabilize Kelley. Davis grabbed Jimmy's phone and scrolled down to find Caitlin's number, Kelley's fiancée, before she caught wind of the situation on a breaking news story. He handed the phone to Ashley as it began to ring. Their eyes met for a moment. Their fingers brushed. It was all the reassurance she needed to keep herself from shattering.

Ashley reached Caitlin on the second ring and told her to meet them at the hospital. There was the panic of a terrified lover on the other side of the call, but Ashley did what she could to reassure her.

"Let's wait until the docs check him out before our imagination runs wild," Ashley was saying. She heard a sharp scream, and the phone line went dead.

The Bronco pulled up outside the hospital as the EMS was making room. They left the car in the circular entrance of the emergency driveway and threw a **POLICE BUSINESS** placard on the dashboard. After flying through the first set of doors, they were abruptly stopped by a nurse trailing the team that was racing Kelley up to surgery.

The officers were told they could go no further and were directed into a waiting area outside the surgical suites. Now it was a waiting game. This was one of those "been there, done that, this sucks" experiences. They paced and waited for Caitlyn and what would seem like endless hours until they would be given answers.

Rick busied himself getting ready for his meeting with Julian Gando. As he put on his neatly pressed Ralph Lauren suit, a fleeting memory of Brandi entered his subconscious. He remembered getting dressed for a date with her. It seems that since his vacation in St. Maartin, she had been creeping into his thoughts. Actually since before then. What had first put the memory of her back into his mind? Was it the reunion? He laughed, thinking he needed another vacation, especially after the past week's horror.

Ralph's was a fourth generation eatery located in the heart of South Philadelphia on Ninth Street. Over its history it has fed such celebrities as Roosevelt, Frank Sinatra, Rocky Marciano, and many others who wanted to feast on old family recipes. It was Gando's favorite place outside his New York haunts.

When Rick arrived, Julian Gando was at the bar having his seven and seven, a throwback drink not too unlike himself. Gando had grown up in Brooklyn in a large family with six brothers and sisters. His middle sister's wedding could have been taken straight out of the wedding scene in *Goodfellas,* except, unlike the movie, everyone's name wasn't Paul or Mary. He had worked as a union negotiator for many years, although his job description was unclear. One thing was certain though; there had never been any labor unrest in any of his unions. His reputation was impeccable, although means to an end were not always clear. He was a genuinely nice guy but was also someone who had to be shown respect and told the blunt truth about everything. Trying to deceive Gando was known to have dire consequences, although none were ever proven.

Gando had met Rick and Carl a dozen or so years ago when he'd needed to host a clandestine meeting in Atlantic City. That particular meeting helped cement Gando's reputation when one of the guests "slipped" off the penthouse balcony on the forty-fifth floor. Witnesses would later say it was an odd scene, watching a man doing the Australian crawl with no water beneath him. It was also bizarre that not a single guest had noticed his mishap until the screaming was heard ten floors below. As one may assume, no charges were filed against any of the partygoers.

The two powerhouses of New York and Philadelphia greeted each other with the stereotypical Hollywood embrace and shoulder slap.

"Pleasure to see you, and on time too. Hope that little cocktail I slipped you for Carl a few weeks ago came in handy," Julian stated.

"As always, you're a saint," Rick replied.

"Let's get a table. The aroma of garlic has woken up my appetite," Gando joked.

The waiter took them upstairs to a second-level table with a sidewalk view of Ninth Street. The waiter took their drink order, Rick having his usual brandy, but it would be only one, he reminded himself. Gando refreshed his seven and seven and the waiter mentioned the specials before departing.

They briefly discussed the menu, Rick touting the sautéed long hots if Gando liked the spicy peppers. Along with the mussels in red sauce, an agreement had been reached.

When the waiter returned, he paced a small bread basket out along with their drinks. Gando ordered the two appetizers along with a medium rare veal chop with mushrooms, one of the signature dishes. Rick opted for the Veal Rollatine, another house specialty, smothered with prosciutto and mozzarella and bathed in a mushroom wine sauce. With the formalities out of the way and any ears well out of reach for listening in, Gando slid his chair closer.

He hunched over the table and said to Rick, "Let me tell you a story. It is necessary to tell you so something about myself I do not normally share. That way you will get the whole picture. May I continue?"

"You have my undivided attention," Rick said, as if a teacher had just told him to be silent and listen attentively. "Please continue."

"In many ways I'm an old fashioned guy, which is one reason I'm still single at this stage in my life. Part of that reason is that work has been a priority, and I don't feel that it's fair if you can't give your spouse or partner the time needed to enjoy each other. I have had several relationships, most of them failing due to that single fact. And if I need to get laid, I have my friends in New York as well as your glamorous selection right here in Philly. That keeps my physical needs in check, but not the emotional ones. Last year I met a stunning woman in Atlantic City named Bryant Merril. She happens to live up on the Mainline and has a small travel business. It's called *Get Out of Town*. Pretty catchy name, eh, Rick?"

The waiter interrupted with the appetizer course, and Gando pointed to his drink, indicating it was time for a refill. Rick waved his hand, still nursing his.

Gando continued. "I was down in AC on some business and went to play some craps. My attention was immediately drawn to this looker, so I joined the table. She had brunette hair with reddish streaks. Her eyes were hazel, her lips perfect. We started the normal small talk but our eyes kept locking in on each other. I was stricken, and that hasn't happened that often. I called over the pit boss and asked the ladies if they wanted to join me for dinner. With a little girl talk between them, they consented. Since we were at the Taj Mahal, they comped us for dinner at *Il Mulino*. I felt bad for her friend—Adrianna Falcone was the name and a looker too, don't get me wrong—but the two of us talked nonstop. Just like two little kids." Julian paused, smiled, and dabbed some bread into the red sauce.

Rick remained attentive.

Julian continued as he sipped his cocktail. "She grew up near Trenton and went to college over at Villanova, so she's a smart gal. Her dad was an accountant at some Princeton based firm, and her mom worked for the state. I guess that's where all that education came from.

"So she graduates Villanova, specializing in—I mean majoring in— economics and business. During her senior year, she meets some preppy marketing major and falls for the lug. He hits it big with some software firm and they move up to the Mainline out by some town called Devon. They have some type of horse event there or something like that those WASPs follow. Anyways, the marriage is in the crapper within four years. Why the hell get married?"

Rick's thoughts again turned to Brandi. *It's that word love that's stirring up my emotions,* he thought. Rick nodded and asked Julian to continue. He really wasn't sure where this was going.

Dinner arrived, along with the pasta and parmesan. The waiter put the cheese through the mill, and it left a white blanket coating contrasting with the marinara sauce's rich red color. Julian tasted and nodded an approval for the choices.

Rick raised his glass for a toast to a fine meal and profitable business dealings to come. He didn't remember the age old adage, *Be careful what you wish for.*

Julian went on with the story. "So for the past four years he has been an asshole when it comes to the common property settlement. They live in this two million dollar mansion, which has pretty much retained its value, but he's not willing to share it with her. Meanwhile, he runs around with some skanks, stays out with no explanation, and plays poker with the guys once a week. Meanwhile, she stays faithful, wants the divorce to look good, and that's where I come in. We been spending a fair amount of time together, and I really dig this woman. She knows some of what I do but doesn't really want to know, as long as we are honest with everything else."

"So you want me to throw some travel business her way, Julian?" Rick queried.

"You're getting ahead of the story, Rick. Let me continue," he said. "So this prick really doesn't care what she does or what he does. He has threatened her to take the offer, or he will ruin her. What a fuckhead. Here is where we get to the crux of the matter. This divorce can drag on for who knows how long, and that's unacceptable to me. Unlike business, when it comes to matters of the heart, I am not as patient a man."

Rick imagined he was not a patient man in either case but refrained from saying that. He heard an imaginary drum roll in his head. This was why he was here.

"I have an extremely lucrative proposition for you, Rick, so hear me out." Julian's chair slid around the table, sitting even closer now. His voice dropped into a low whisper and he continued. "I do not want to waste *any* time," he said. "He has a three million dollar life insurance policy, and half is yours if you help me solve this problem. Plus I will throw a bonus if the investigation dies a slow death within the first month. I will set up a meet between you and Bryant for the weekend, and she can fill you in on some more of the particulars—his habits, places he goes. When he's alone. The whole nine yards.

"The reasons I have chosen you are twofold. For one thing, you have a reputation as being a trusted, stand-up guy. They say you protect your friends no matter what the cost. That's an admirable trait in my book. Secondly, we both know you are still the main guy in Carl's accident, and with him gone, you're going to lose some business. I'm offering you a lot more than you can expect over the next several years. You know where I'm coming from. I want you for this one."

Rick's transfixed attention was broken as the reality of what he was being asked to do began to sink in.

"I don't need an answer this minute. Explore my proposition and request, please. Call it … leveling a favor. I slipped you that delightful little cocktail; you assist me in this issue." He said it in a serious tone.

"I … I will," Rick replied tentatively.

"I'll call tomorrow at noon. When you meet with Bryant, I know you will process what she tells you and develop a creative plan. Thank you, for listening and for paying close attention, Rick," Julian finished.

Rick smiled back at Julian and offered a "You're welcome" back at him. Inside Rick's head, he was processing what he'd just heard at a mile a second. It was a risk, and murder was not his primary game. One week later and he was still a free man, which did say something about his fastidious planning. He had to weigh the risk against the reward. Hell, he hadn't even made that money over the course of five years, even when Carl was his partner. It also was kind of exciting, as well as being done for what he believed was a just cause.

But the most impending thought he considered was that he wasn't really being asked but rather told that he was accepting this job. So, in actuality, he had to accept. The consequences of refusing a man with Julian's power and connections would be lethal at best. And besides, he didn't know how to fly off a building and didn't want to find out. Julian had been kind enough to offer the Rocuronium *Bromide* when Rick had inquired about a particularly attention-grabbing drug. In essence, he did owe the man for it. When Julian called the next day, Rick knew what the answer was going to be.

The waiter arrived advertising the desserts but both shook their heads in unison, as there was little room left for either of them. Coffee was poured and the conversation turned to the various New York-Philadelphia sports rivalries. It was a subject that had no gray area or any way of convincing the other party how superior one team was to the other. They both laughed as they called it a tie.

They stood, giving the standard masculine departure hug, which closely resembled the meeting embrace they had preformed hours ago. They thanked the maitre d' for the superb experience, headed for the exit, and went their separate ways. Rick thought this might turn out to be a long, sleepless night.

Chapter XVIII

A long time was spent in the waiting area, as many of Jimmy Kelley's fellow officers had shown up to offer their support. He had been in surgery for almost seven hours, with no update given. They did learn the explosion had been a nasty pipe bomb, and some of its contents had penetrated several organs. It would be necessary to repair the life-threatening internal injuries first to stabilize him. The skin on his upper body had been penetrated by high-velocity ball bearings, which had spewed from the weapon when it detonated.

Doctors could make no diagnosis regarding his ability to see or hear until he was conscious, but his eardrums not been ruptured. All in all he was a bloody mess, and his fate was still unknown.

After midnight, two surgeons approached the entourage of friends and family. A tall, thin man, his eyes intense, relayed the message that Jimmy's outcome was still uncertain.

"Let me tell you what has occurred and what we're doing to stabilize him," the lead surgeon said. "Mr. Kelley sustained severe damage to his kidneys and spine. Several of the vertebrae were severed, but we do not know if any degree of paralysis has occurred. His blood pressure and heart rate are stabilized, but he has yet to regain consciousness. The next twelve hours are extremely critical in assessing how his body is adapting to its condition. He is young, in good physical shape, and his heart is strong. We are doing everything humanly possible, so you can all contribute by talking to the Big Guy upstairs. We need all the resources we can get. I'll alert you if we see any critical changes. Go home, rest, and leave it in our capable hands."

With that, Caitlin broke down again, as she had all through the day and night. She and Jimmy's friends were a comforting source of strength and hope. The doctor was right. There was nothing left they could do but conserve their sanity in these hard times.

Rick tossed and turned with a restless urge, needing to convince himself he was doing the necessary thing beyond any reasonable doubt. He needed to know this guy's habits, his most visible friends, and his ironclad routines. He needed to know a lot, but this would not be possible until after he met with Bryant on Friday.

He impulsively rose from the bed and headed to the bathroom. He swung open the medicine cabinet and removed two valiums from an amber prescription container. He dry-swallowed the pair and headed back to bed. He knew two would render him into a restful REM. They always did.

At six the next morning Davis's cell phone rang once before he answered. He was already awake, not being able to sleep for any extended period of time. It was Caitlin calling to say Kelley's condition had worsened and she was heading over to the hospital. She needed to be close so that her prayers would be better heard.

Davis hopped out of bed and showered and quickly shaved. Five minutes later he headed to the lobby, got into his car, and headed for the hospital.

As Davis drove, a laundry list of items filled his head. This investigation was the only priority. He had to analyze all of the explosive evidence, hopefully learning where the bomb's components had originated. He would bring the ATF in on this one. They could also research if any similar devices had been constructed, by whom, and when they had been used, looking for patterns. He also needed the team to follow up on the two bodies that had been found at the scene. Who were their enemies? What had they done? Why were they at the club? Who would want them dead? Eventually these would all be entered in his notebook.

Davis removed the cell phone from his pocket and sent a text. He asked the other eight team members to meet at the conference room at 1:00 p.m. to review the recent events. He knew they would all be ready. He headed toward the ICU in order to meet Caitlin and get the latest updates. As he strode down the hallway, he looked up and saw her waiting. Her eyes were pink circles and she looked meek, standing with her hands at her side, shoulders hunched and head down. He knew from the behavioral science study she was showing the sign of helplessness and fear. He had to approach her being positive.

"Thanks for the call. Have they told you anything yet?" he asked.

"A nurse told me to wait here and the surgeon would speak to me. That was twenty minutes ago."

"It's a full moon and there are probably lots of accidents and deaths. This is the infamous City of Brotherly Love, you know."

A faint smiled crossed her lips.

The doctor approached, the look on his face unreadable. There were no positive or negative signs that Davis could interpret. They shook hands and the doctor got right to the point. Davis liked that.

"We're going to have to take him back in. Some debris we thought was inconsequential was not. If we remove it, it will decrease some internal swelling and bleeding. He is still unconscious, but all his vitals are as good as can be expected. He's a fighter, and that will carry a lot of weight in the hours to come. We'll have him for a while, so take a break and check in around one." The doctor gave off an air of confidence, which was so needed at this moment.

Davis grabbed Kelley's fiancé's hand and led her toward the elevator. "Go down to the cafeteria or take a walk. Sitting here is not productive. You must stay positive. I'll meet you back here whenever you call. I have a team meeting, and this case is top priority. You don't fuck with our team. We *will* find out who is responsible."

He kissed her on the cheek and headed to the garage to get his car. Along the way back to the office, Davis planned to stop to ask a fairly reliable street informant if there was any gossip about this case. He drove down to Broad and Catherine but Sid still wasn't around. He circled several square blocks and came up empty. He couldn't waste any more time, so he headed back to the office to begin solving this case.

When he arrived at conference room C, the flip chart and multicolored markers were waiting for him. Besides the team members, a familiar face was smiling from the back of the room. It was Henry

Barkin, an ATF agent Stephen had worked with on several cases over the past several years. He knew it must have been Ashley who'd called him in. Funny how she had a way of reading his mind. When he noticed Henry, he called the meeting to order.

"Thanks to all of you for the diligence and dedication you have shown over the past two incidents." Davis continued in an upbeat manner. "I want to tell you a quick story and introduce you all to an interim team member who came all the way up from DC to help with the case. His name's Henry Barkin, but you may all call him Hank the Yank, as I do."

Davis went on to tell the story of their first meeting. Henry, or Hank as he preferred, was a born and bred true-blue New Yorker, which is not the most loved visitor in the working class town of Philadelphia. He was a diehard Yankee fan, and when Davis met him, some friendly friction had ensued.

When David learned Hank was a fan of Yankees third baseman Alex Rodriguez, he taunted him and asked, "*What would A-Rod do for you if you were out of work? Would he put food on the table and take care of your family?*" This was the same dialogue from *A Bronx Tale*.

Hank replied, "*Nah, he wouldn't do nothin' for me. Don't you know? Nobody cares!*"

And that completed the scene, creating an immediate bond—a "guy thing." They'd stayed in touch ever since.

Davis grabbed a white-board marker and started writing a list of investigative priorities:

1. Follow up on the forensic evidence (shell casings, fingerprints, etc.).

2. Hank: Bomb components, any similar devices used, etc.

3. Recanvass neighbors for witnesses, unusual noises, or people.

4. Phone traces on the two victims, both of whom had been identified.

5. Drew Hutzer: Point man who will coordinate all incoming data.

6. Geek: Any data or phone traces from electronics found at scene.

He went on to mention that the Carl Mickels case was on hold, and Jimmy's was priority one. These cases may be tied together somehow, but it was too early to presume. Overtime would not be an issue, which was a rarity in the cash-strapped city that was closing libraries and public services. This was one of their own, and no expenses were to be spared.

After an hour or so of spirited discussion and insights, Davis ended the meeting, and the team departed to start their assignments.

Davis headed back to the hospital after receiving Caitlin's call. The doctor was due to see her soon, and she wanted Davis there. She was confused and scared. She was submissive to a certain degree and needed a strong-willed body for much needed support. His timing was uncanny, arriving almost at the same time as the doctor. Again the surgeon's face gave no expression of what he was about to say.

"Thank you both for meeting me. I'll get to the point. We removed the obstruction, and his neurological scans are improving. We still don't know when he'll regain consciousness, but the sooner the better. I encourage you, Caitlin, to talk to him. Medical man or not, I do think it helps. His monitors will alert the nurses if there is a critical emergency, but all we can do is wait. That's all I have."

With that short synopsis, the doctor headed back to his beeping pager and left them alone. It was going to be yet another long evening.

Chapter XIX

Rick began to dress and prepare for his meeting with his new assignment, Bryant Merril. He was more anxious than nervous, having never been in a similar situation. He put on a comfortable pair of khakis, a new Izod golf shirt, and a pair of black loafers. He walked over to the kitchen table and slid the contents out of his bag. Six disposable cell phones appeared on the countertop. He fixed a white adhesive label to three of them. The A was for all calls to Abbey. B was strictly for all calls going to Bryant, and the G was for Gando. The other phones would be used as needed, with his personal BlackBerry for all legal business dealings as well as being his contact number.

He picked up the phone labeled B and dialed the number from memory. On the first ring, a nervous Bryant picked up the phone and softly said, "Hello."

"This is a friend of a friend," Rick said assuredly. "I would hope we can meet for dinner tonight and talk over old times and new."

"That would be lovely. Where would you like to meet?"

"I was told you enjoy good steaks, so how does Sullivan's sound?"

"You were correctly informed; sounds like a date."

He was trying to ease some of the tension that he detected in her voice. "Make an 8:00 p.m. reservation under the name Williams. Does that work for you?"

"Yes, that works for me," she said, her voice sounding a bit more at ease.

"Then eight it shall be. See you then." Rick pushed the end button and tossed the cell back on the table.

He knew he'd have to make her feel confident and at ease with what was going to happen. He would need much information about her husband in order to get away with the murder and investigation that would follow. He also didn't want to wait too long, to make Julian happy as well as to get paid. He smiled and thought, *The first was tough—the second, and last, will be easier.* He walked over to the bottle of Knob Creek and poured a double. He raised it to his lips, tilted his head, and inhaled the bronze liquid in one movement.

As Caitlin sat on the edge of the bed, she firmly held Jimmy's hand as she spoke softly to him. She apologized for all the hard times, as well as promised him the best when he came out of it. Her attitude was positive, just as the doctor had suggested. As she went to stand up, she released her grip around Jimmy's fingers. She was startled when she saw his fingers move in a beckoning fashion. She wasn't sure if she was hallucinating, but then his body twisted slightly, and she knew she wasn't. She grabbed the nurses' call button on the bed and repeatedly plunged it down. Tears were welling in her eyes as two nurses arrived in the room. She told them what had happened, and one picked up the room phone to have the doctor paged.

"I know he moved," Caitlin said excitedly.

The nurses then heard a faint moan come from the patient, along with another twitch. They checked the monitor, noticing the vitals were much improved over the last reading.

"This is a good sign," said the one with Amanda on her name tag.

The doctor arrived and checked the charts and monitors. It was many tedious minutes of intense physical evaluation before at last a faint smile appeared. Then, turning to Caitlin, he gave a nod and said, "We have passed what I believe to be a critical stage. I think he'll beat this."

She hugged the doctor as the tears began to flow more freely. He stepped away and released her, telling her to make some calls and share the good news with his friends.

He left the room, knowing it had been touch and go all the way until this moment.

Rick pulled up to the valet entrance of Sullivan's and slid out of the driver seat. The valet made a comment about how awesome his classic car was, nodding in admiration. He smiled and slipped the guy a five. The valet thanked him several times, waving his hand as he got in the car, assuring he would take care of his baby.

He entered the crowded restaurant and ducked into the bar area. His eyes surveyed the crowd, a combination of self-centered yuppies, old money, and wanna-bees. He noticed an attractive woman, a looker as Julian called her, sitting on a bar stool near the window and occasionally peering out. He approached the table and subtly spoke.

"Excuse me, Mrs. Merril, but is this seat taken?"

Her look of surprise told him he had been correct in identifying her, as she'd had no way of recognizing him. She stood up and offered her hand, formally introducing herself. "It's a pleasure, Mr. Williams. Will you please join me?" She swept a hand to indicate the spot open beside her at the bar.

"I would love to, Mrs. Merril. Would you like a drink?"

"A cosmo would be great. Our table should be ready in fifteen minutes, according to the hostess. She's a blonde, so let's see if she can tell time."

Rick smiled. *She even has a sense of humor. Julian's got a keeper here.*

The drinks arrived, and Rick threw down a twenty and a five. He gave the "keep the change" hand signal, and the waitress thanked him and smiled. They made small talk, Bryant mentioning that she had gone to school at Villanova after growing up on the other side of the Delaware River in Lawrenceville. He mentioned he was a true blue Philadelphia native, born and bred. There was no other place he would rather live. They both agreed it was a good place to live.

The hostess rapidly approached their table, appearing like a woman whose only mission in life was to shuttle guests off to their designated dinner seats. They arose from the side table, Rick imitating her motion as Bryant smirked and followed. Rick was doing his best to raise Bryant's comfort level and lower any uneasiness she may be feeling.

They were escorted to a table in the rear, which had only one neighbor within ear shot. Rick didn't think it mattered so much as he observed three empty bottles of wine and an unopened bottle of Cristal on the table.

They slid into the leather booth, settling close enough to talk yet far enough apart to keep it business-like. He handed her a menu, indicating they would get the order out of the way and less time to be interrupted.

The waiter, introducing himself as Raymond, asked if they needed their drinks to be refreshed. They both nodded, and he scribbled the order on his check. The barmaid would convey to that particular server what they had been drinking, a nice little touch. He asked if they wanted the same and they nodded again.

He returned very shortly and placed the drinks at the respective places. He queried whether they would like to hear the specials, and Rick answered he would. He was getting tired of nodding. Nothing on the list of fresh catches or the stuffed veal chop caught either's fancy. Bryant spoke first, ordering a spinach salad and an eight-ounce filet, medium rare. Rick followed, opting for a jumbo lump crab cake, mentioning it *had* to be shared, and a one-pound medium-rare rib eye, his favorite.

After the waiter left, Rick raised his drink and lowered his head to speak. "I have known and worked with Julian for a number of years. He's a good man, very respected and honest, a real stand-up kind of man. What I'm undertaking is not my usual line of work. Julian specifically asked me to do this favor, and I would never refuse his requests." Rick noticed an intense and attentive expression on Bryant's face, a sign that she paid attention. Attention usually went hand in hand with those who treated certain matters with a serious nature. That was good, he thought.

Rick continued. "Tonight I will need to learn a good deal about your husband. Things such as habits, friends, and places he goes. I will need any schedules he keeps on a daily or weekly basis. I will need to know what kind of car or cars he drives, where he works, parks, goes for lunch and the like. Until I can formulate a plan of action, I will not rush into anything that can direct blame or culpability toward you. You will know nothing about what I'm doing or when. Nor will he."

Bryant smiled and released a breath, along with the tension she had been experiencing. She sipped her cosmo and waited for Rick to speak.

"One thing I'm a stickler about is trails. By this I mean paper, electronic, or leaving clues. There will be no DNA evidence within one hundred miles of any of us. We may only talk once or twice more, and then you will never hear from me or see me again. Same goes for Julian. He will be conveniently out of town when this happens, and I'm only assuming that your affair has been pretty discreet. I will leave it to Julian to handle the financial end of this deal, and I trust him implicitly. I also have a good feeling about your discretion, which confirms my confidence in you." With his conclusion, he lifted his glass as a toast, and their glasses met halfway.

Over the course of their dinner, Bryant spoke as Rick listened attentively, asking clarifying questions on occasion. His memory was without reproach, one of his best attributes. After a third drink refill, Bryant's information flowed in a steady stream of useful facts about her husband's routine. She added that she thought he was seeing some bitch on a nonregular basis but could always tell the moment he came home. He attended a steady card game, had dinner meetings for new clients on a monthly basis, and went to an occasional sporting event or office function. He worked for a large brokerage account on the Mainline, and his attitude reflected his snobbishness. She explained that that was one of the numerous reasons they were having dinner together. He fully understood where she was coming from.

"By the way, his full name is Harrington Alexander Marcus the third," she said, smiling.

"Hell, did you have to marry a guy whose name takes up two full lines in the phone book?" he chided gleefully.

"His friends call him Ham because of his initials and his good friends, stressing the word *good*, may call him Harry. I personally prefer 'Asshole.'"

Bryant was unknowingly convincing him of her disdain for the man. Although she must have been in love at some time, those feelings had dissipated, and Julian was her new significant other.

The waiter arrived for the end game of dinner and asked if they wanted to see the dessert tray. Neither expressed much excitement, and the waiter, reading their expressions, ascertained that it was a no. They nodded, and he said he would return with the check. Before they rose to leave, Rick slid a slip of paper containing a number into her palm. He asked her to call him if she remembered anything else that would be of use to him.

"Please memorize the number and destroy the paper when you're done, Bryant."

She agreed, and they stepped out into the balmy evening air.

Chapter XX

The next morning Davis woke with a positive attitude. His laptop had relayed a message that the two victims of the South Philadelphia homicide had been identified but also mentioned that the information would not be sent on an unsecure network. The information awaited him at his Roundhouse office. Before he headed to work he wanted to stop at the hospital and pay a visit to Kelley. His morning ritual of a shave and shower were hurried along. The elevator was already at his floor, so he knew his stars were in alignment. He jogged to his car, fit the keys in the ignition, and started out.

In another part of town, Rick Grosse was starting the day early too. The morning news was jammed with information about a car bombing that had nearly killed some officer on the OCTF, Davis's division. He realized that when one of the task force who was investigating Carl's case was critically injured, it would take precedence over his homicide investigation, which gave Rick some breathing room. For the next several days he would be following Harrington and keeping a dossier of his travels, contacts, and habits. He had to balance the expediency of the hit along with the safety factor. Hell, he couldn't spend the money if he was convicted of life without parole. He also brought a small tape recorder with an ear bud, in case he had to follow on foot. He was a thorough, careful man.

Davis made a quick stop at the Wawa next to the hospital. He filled up a twenty-ounce cup with hazelnut cream coffee, along with a breakfast sandwich stuffed into a cardboard box. He grabbed a Kit Kat bar for Kelley, in case he was up to it. The kid loved those bars.

He rode the elevator up to the ICU. Upon entering the room, he noticed that Geek, Ashley, and Ellen Sue were all bedside. Kelley lay partially propped up on several pillows but was still connected to a maze of colored tubes.

He wore a hint of a smile when Davis approached. Davis leaned in, inches from Kelley's ear. "I brought you a Kit Kat. Now would you like for me to feed it to you too?" he joked in his usual manner.

Kelley emitted a barely audible whisper. "Fuck you. Don't make me get out of this bed."

The crowd appreciated his retort, and all nodded in approval.

"Get them yet?" Kelley asked.

"Not yet, buddy, but it's the number-one priority of the team. The feds have loaned us Hank from ATF for as long as we need him. You betcha it'll get solved."

The team carried on some brief banter until a nurse came in and requested they all get back to work and catch some bad guys, or maybe it was a ploy to get them to get lost.

Davis called a nine o' clock meeting to discuss the new developments. With that, they all headed for their respective vehicles and another fact-finding powwow back at the station.

Rick drove up the Schuylkill Expressway, barely beating the heavily congested morning rush-hour traffic. He bared left off the ramp toward Route 1 south, braking at the first red light. He drove several more blocks to the Bala Office Complex and turned in. Harrington's Lexus had yet to arrive, which meant perfect timing on his part. Moments later, Harrington arrived and exited the car, but not before he hand-brushed his blond cropped hair and fussed with the lower button on his navy-blue Armani blazer. Rick really hated these preppy, pretty-boy types. He folded his right arm over his black leather briefcase and vanished behind two large glass doors. Rick recorded the time, parking location and decided it was OK to run up to the diner for breakfast.

David arrived first, around 8:30 a.m., giving him ample time to peruse the several reports that covered his desk. The first was in a green folder marked **INTERPOL**. This immediately caught his attention, as he had never seen such a folder. Upon opening the folder, he scanned the name in the center of the page. It read **Uri Petronov**. Several color and black-and-white photos were paperclipped to the inside of the jacket. They matched the victim down to the crude prison tattoos on his neck. Reading the report, he learned that Petronov had spent more than ten years in prison, his crimes ranging from assault to racketeering to attempted murder. His age read twenty-four. The report went on to say that he was not tied to any one crime boss but was contracted out by several of the major criminal enterprises that had blossomed after the Soviet breakup.

Davis pulled his pad closer and began to jot down his thoughts. *Why a Russian shot in the middle of Italian controlled south Philly? Was he being contracted out? Was he just a messenger or was he making some threats?* He was a totally unknown player in the city's ethnic crimes divisions. The Russians had a presence in northeast Philadelphia but were known to conduct their business below the radar. He would bring this up at the meeting.

The next file contained some of the particulars found at the crime scene. These items included the hardware released by the explosive device as well as the weapons found on the two dead Russians. All would be traced for prints, serial numbers, and to determine whether the weapons had been used in previous crimes. This would be Hank's area of expertise.

The third file contained information on the inside dealings of the Russian mob, along with their current areas of illegal pursuits. These included activities where they had a foothold, such as in numbers, protection, prostitution, and fraud within consumer affairs. Several years ago indictments had come down, accusing Russian mobs of shorting consumers at the gas pumps, shaving two ounces off per gallon. It didn't sound like much, but if five hundred cars filled up with fifteen gallons on the average, profits would be about fifty dollars per pump. If a station had six pumps, it became three hundred. Multiplied by several hundred stations, the profits could be staggering. This was only one example of

Russian ingenuity at its finest. Davis glanced up at the wall clock, which read 8:59 a.m.

He closed the folders, not being able to finish the last few, and approached the conference area. *Let the games begin*, he thought.

Chapter XXI

Rick rose from his booth prior to his breakfast's arrival. He dug inside his pocket for some quarters and slipped outside the diner, feeding four quarters into the red newspaper dispenser containing the *Daily News*. Breakfast always tasted better if the *Daily News* was served as a side dish. He leafed through the first six pages. Other than one story on the political climate at city hall, the rest of the stories highlighted a brazen bank robbery, a woman who was found dead at her residence with sixty-seven cats wandering the premises, and a drive-by that injured a twelve-year-old boy. There was the update citing the ongoing investigation regarding the death of two Russian nationals and the recovering Jim Kelley, now deemed a Philadelphia hero. Nothing more on the death of Carl Mickels, which confirmed that life was good.

As the waitress slid his breakfast across the Formica tabletop, a vibration alerted his attention. He reached into his pants pocket for the phone. It was phone B, that of Bryant Merril. Rick answered the phone in an almost abrupt yet not-too-concerned manner.

"Yes, dear, what's up?"

"It's my husband again," she began. "He says he has an important business meeting down at the Trump and is not sure when he'll be home. He told me not to wait up for him."

"I understand," he responded. "I can follow his thinking. Don't worry. I'll look into it."

In English, Rick understood he was leaving shortly for a trip to Atlantic City. He would scarf down the rest of his breakfast, get back to his office, and start the journey. He paid the check and drove back to wait for Harrington to leave.

The ride down to Atlantic City via the AC Expressway was an hour of boring scenery with the occasional overpriced toll. Deer carcasses were scattered along the route, the result of the ever-expanding population in the Garden State. Blueberry bogs and corn rows were interspersed along the highway, along with occasional signs reminding that not wearing a seat belt is a punishable offense. Rick smiled. *So is murder.*

He sped up and exited into the heart of Atlantic City, the glittering lights of Caesar's Palace illuminating the afternoon haze. He turned left and followed Arctic Avenue for several blocks. Turning right at the sign for the Taj, he drove the two blocks and handed the car over to a waiting valet. He strode through the heavy glass doors and waited for Harrington to arrive. He assumed he would take the same entrance rather than self park.

Twenty minutes later Harrington entered the lobby with the look of a man on a mission. He circled the edge of the casino floor, Rick keeping a safe distance behind. Harrington turned left at the bar/nightclub entrance and took a vacant seat at the oval bar. The lounge had a multitude of television sets, all tuned in to various sports shows. The bar was topped off with video poker machines, filling almost every square foot of the cavernous casino with games of chance.

Rick took a seat with a semiobstructed view of his subject, who seemed oblivious to all that surrounded him. He removed a cigar from its tube and lit it up. Several minutes later, a striking blonde approached him, and his smile widened. She kissed his neck, ran her fingers through the back of his hair, and sat down. He summoned the bartender, who happened to be one of Rick's acquaintances, Richie Fontaine. Richie had bet some sports with Rick, much to Rick's dismay. Richie was amazing at picking college football and won more than he lost. Not a good business practice, so Rick passed him and a couple of losers on to one of his buddies in the business.

Rick observed the couple during the time they spent at the bar. Rick figured it was one of his regulars, maybe a call girl, but it was obvious this was not their first encounter. He would call Abbey later with a description to see if Abbey was familiar with her.

He glanced back toward them. They had gotten up and were heading toward the elevators. This was the end of the surveillance, Rick knew. The casino had more video cameras than Best Buy and he didn't want to be seen anywhere near the couple. The day was done and not a total waste. But it did give him a better sense of who Harrington was, as well as deepen his disdain for the man. Although Rick had never been married, he never cheated on any of his steadies and didn't care for those who did.

Rick waited until they were out of sight until he left the bar. He wasn't in a gambling mood, so he headed for the exit and his car. An hour and change later, he was back at his condo in Philly. Before bed he went over the day's events in his mind, took a Xanax, and went to bed.

The day at the Roundhouse was turning out to be quite productive. Davis doled out a multitude of assignments on the investigation. Several new faces filled the room. The higher ups had made this a high priority case, adding some other investigators from various departments.

The first group was assigned the Russian angle. He wanted to know if any joint ventures had been initiated between the two varied crime factions. A greater possibility was if there was going to be a turf war for control of activities such as protection, prostitution, gambling, or drugs. Philadelphians were a hard lot who supported those illegal acts with the verve of Rocky Balboa.

The second team would concentrate on all forensic information gathered to date. The endless wealth of technology available in Washington needed to be explored in an effort to come up with a suspect. They could research similar crimes for patterns such as bombings using similar components, as well as check fingerprint files available at a national level.

The third team would recanvass the area, gathering video surveillance tapes that may have focused on the area surrounding the crime scene. Here they could capture license plates, look for anything out of the ordinary, and interview people in businesses and residences. Geek would be the point man, creating a timeline and synopsis of the event. His computer skills were so advanced, he could create videos of different scenarios that gave new perspectives to the case.

Davis decided they would reconvene in several days and continue the task of putting together all gathered information.

They were heading into the weekend again. He had a date—of sorts. After canceling on his brother the weekend before, Davis knew this time he had to see him. Michael may have been an understanding person, but when his only entertainment consisted of odd jobs in national security and the bimonthly brotherly visit, Davis always felt guilty not showing.

Case files in tow, Stephen Davis headed for his office door. He gave one last glance around the office as if in the hopes to see Ashley Stone with the signature smile on her lips.

Chapter XXII

The next several evenings Rick trailed Harrington like a dark shadow. He needed to find the opportunity and place that offered the least amount of risk with the greatest amount of reward. Nothing had presented itself yet, but tonight was the man's poker night, and Rick may have found his opening.

Rick had switched cars, borrowing Abbey's nondescript black Ford Taurus since his Mazda stood out a bit more than he liked. He followed Harrington to a side street off City Line Avenue. The house ended up not being a Mainline-type McMansion he'd expected a high-stakes game might be played in. In general all Mainlines were topnotch, snot-don't-stick places filled with upper-crust wealthy who were too rich to deign to walk on pavement.

The smaller homes were for the next few rungs down the wealth ladder. At least this area had sidewalks, even if they were never used. The street was populated with single detached homes, which were old but decently valued due to the size of the property, which typically meant a three-foot patch of grass mowed twice weekly with a riding lawn mower. The streets were dimly lit and only blocks from the edge of the city limits, which was a higher crime area. This was good.

Harrington pulled his car into an available spot and Rick drove by, circled the block, and pulled into a spot several cars behind Harrington's. Rick knew the card game started at eight and would last until midnight or so. The Phillies weren't playing, so it would be a boring evening of sitting alone in the car.

Over the past several days Rick had been doing lots of thinking and soul searching regarding many aspects of his life. He was about to commit a murder and was not sure why. There was the obvious financial gain. It was also a favor, as well as "an offer he couldn't refuse." He also was not a fan of the type of person Harrington was—a cocky, spoiled Mainline brat who didn't know how to treat a woman. Regardless of the reason, he was a man of his word and would follow through with his promise and duties.

It would be three or four more hours before the card game would break up, and he would see if his plan could still be put into effect. He exited the car, as its location was just where he wanted it to be. He grabbed his unread *Philadelphia Inquirer,* the city's other daily, and walked toward one of his favorite delicatessens. For dessert, he hoped he would have the opportunity to finish his job.

While Rick had been following his prey, a major break had risen in the case that had been consuming Davis's team. During the early afternoon, a tip had come in from one of the squad's confidential informers. Word on the street was that these two crazy, connected Russian dudes were coming down from the Big Apple to settle a score. Rumor had it that a bunch of Philadelphia wise guys had gone up there to party and ended up at a whorehouse in Brighton Beach. When it came time to leave, the Philly boys demanded a complimentary pass on the services that had been rendered. Heated words were exchanged, knives came out, and the Russian "pimps" were beaten up and cut, one lying at a local hospital in critical condition. The Philly boys laughed it up and took the two-hour ride down the New Jersey Turnpike back to South Philly. Two members of the team were heading in the opposite direction, up to the Brooklyn hospital to interview the victim. Several calls to the Brooklyn precinct had yielded sketchy information, as the Russians liked to take care of their own problems, and the incident wasn't even reported. The hospital had reported the knife wound, as is protocol with violent crimes.

Davis figured that one of the two victims of the South Philadelphia shootings had been a Russian sent down to extract revenge. He wondered if the Russians were the ones who had planted the bomb that had nearly killed Kelley. *If they did, why did it explode after the incident? They couldn't have detonated the device after they'd been shot—was it on a timer? Or did another individual remain at the scene, detonating it to confuse everybody?* The fact was, this was likely an act of revenge, and he needed to put all the disjointed puzzle pieces together.

When a member of the team came into the conference room B, he was clutching a videotape that contained another answer. The investigators sat around an antique VHS player, turned on the power, and slipped in the black plastic cassette. The tape had been retrieved from a camera mounted on the awning of a pawn shop, set up across the street from the social club. The tape was fast forwarded to a scene that revealed a white van pulling away from the curb. Seconds later the explosion occurred.

Was the bomb detonated by the driver in the van? If so, why? Although the license plate numbers were only partially visible due to the camera angle, they did pick up the red, white, and blue colors of a New York tag. They had a tidbit, a small clue they could incorporate along with the other facts of the case. The video also revealed the Ford logo on rear door panel, along with a smudge of green paint. They would call New York DMV, inquiring about commercial white Ford vans within the five boroughs of New York City. Hopefully they could also get an approximate year from the partial photo. The case was taking larger steps as time went by. Now they had to learn who had set it off, as no timer in any of the bomb debris had been found by the ATF.

Rick entered the deli, the smell of smoked meats and fish permeating the air. He sat at a window table, his normal routine, and ordered what he had come in for, along with some sour pickles. A light foggy mist was beginning to form outside, along with those popular intermittent showers. He grabbed a copy of the *Philadelphia Inquirer,* which the last diner had left behind. He had already dissected the sports section, so he turned to the front section. The paper itself contained four sections, including international and big-time local issues, the regional section, sports, and the featured articles relating to everyday life.

He flipped through the first several pages, noticing articles about the economy, mid-East fighting, and the failure of local politicos to bridge the budget gaps. On page eleven, an article jumped off the page.

Peaceful Caribbean Island Erupts in Violence.

The so-called "friendly island" of St. Maartin was awakened by early morning violence, as local authorities battled a group of suspected drug traffickers with intense gunfire. The island, which has recently become a jumping-off point for South American cartels' cocaine trade was discovered by an undercover source. Two law enforcement officers were fatally wounded, along with eight of the nine suspects. Seven males and one female were killed in a heavy exchange of gunfire in Simpson Bay, a resort area several miles outside Princess Juliana International Airport. A large, undisclosed amount of American and French currency, along with fifty kilograms of cocaine was discovered in plasticized sealed porcelain vases. It was the largest bust in the island's history, and names are being withheld pending further investigation.

Several small photos of the deceased accompanied the article. Rick's gaze was affixed upon a somewhat small photo that may or may not have been Esperanza. Further investigation on his laptop would possibly yield a more precise photo, as well as the actual events.

Rick's imagination went into overdrive as he began to formulate a theory about his past visit to the island, along with the death of his friend and associate, Claude.

He began to theorize that Esperanza, his new confidant, had planned her entry to gain Claude's trust and eventually commandeer his successful business operations. It made sense. He concluded Claude had not been a target and the murder had been staged to eliminate his involvement in the operations. This group of thieves was actually out to steal his connections and contacts in order to expand his market. Anyone who had prior dealings with him was to be dropped, and a new clientele would replace the old, on a much larger and more ambitious scale.

A far as Rick was concerned, it worked. Rick had decided after the killing that he was out of the picture forever. There were other vacation spots in the aquamarine sea, and Rick had a new business plan anyway.

It was only a theory, but it damned well made sense.

His sandwich arrived, breaking his train of thought. The taste of the warm and satisfying sandwich brought back memories of his childhood. His family had come here for years. It was part of his past and of a happier, less complicated time. Rick coated some fries with ketchup and savored his comforting dinner. His mind revving up again, his thoughts turned to the business at hand. He had a plan to take care of Harrington, and he believed it was a good one. If the stars were in alignment, Harrington would be dead before the morning's early editions hit the newsstands.

Chapter XXIII

Rick finished leafing through the paper and checked his watch. The intensity of the rain had increased, and its random sound glancing off the window momentarily hypnotized him. It coincided with the randomness of both Rick's life and his actions. The recurring theme of his lack of direction seemed to unnerve him more and more as of late. It had begun with the high school reunion at the Phillies game, and there was no end in sight. Maybe fate would forge a path—*and if I'm being followed?* He shook his head vigorously, as if to bring himself back to the present and the task at hand. He motioned the waiter for the check and left his usual generous tip. At least that still brought him pleasure. He left the restaurant and headed back to his car.

The fax machine at the Roundhouse continually hummed, delivering a stream of paper relating to the investigation at hand. There were more than thirty vans in the metropolitan area that fit the description they had inquired about. Out of those thirty, three were registered to Russian businesses or individuals, two in the Brighton Beach section of Brooklyn. While two of the task force members were nearing the Verrazano Bridge, connecting Staten Island to Brooklyn, Geek was on the horn talking to a captain by the name of Melitto at the sixtieth precinct. His was the man in charge of the crime scene.

Both the team from Philadelphia's OCTF and the Brooklyn police were simultaneously driving to one of the registered vehicle's location on Twelfth Street.

Davis was in constant contact with the first team. The name on the vehicle registration was Andre Petronov, the last name coinciding with one of the victims found in South Philly. When his team arrived, they found a van with Russian print stenciled on the side. It was green printing, the same color as the small paint mark found on the rear of the van in the video. Davis was a master planner, as one of the agents he sent to New York was a Russian expatiate, fluent in several Russian dialects. To most of Anglophones, the letters appeared to be backward, containing English symbols and punctuation. But to Davis's man, it was immediately recognizable.

"Davis, the van belongs to a company that does electrical work and plumbing, servicing both residential and commercial accounts."

Davis smiled and replied, "Do you think someone with that area of expertise might also know how to construct an explosive device?"

The answer was obvious, as was the gut feeling Davis had when he heard the translation.

Within moments an unmarked van pulled up, the side door slid open, and several SWAT team members dressed in full tactical body armor filed out. The leader pointed to the residence that was located above the storefront marked **Petronov Heating and Plumbing Supply.** The store was dark, so the team entered from an adjacent door that led to the upstairs residence.

The Philly boys left their car and approached the van with weapons drawn. They circled the van. It was locked. Planning was everything, and a search warrant would momentarily arrive from some poor Brooklyn judge rousted out of bed by order of Homeland Security. After all, it was related to a bombing by a foreign group and had killed two Americans. Nothing was overlooked.

As the SWAT team entered the residence, their headsets gave a play-by-play of their activities.

"Front room clear," came one voice.

"Kitchen and bedroom clear. Someone's been here. Lots of papers littering the room, drawers open. Room has been breached."

"Bathroom clear. No occupants or bodies visible," came a third voice.

An official–looking, dark, late-model car pulled up, and two suits exited, holding a folded paper that was assumed to be a search warrant.

One of the men approached the Philly team. "The warrant includes the residence, place of business, and any vehicles clearly connected to the resident or business. Go ahead and search the van."

Gibson, one of the OCTF team, and Chekov, on loan from a separate division, grabbed a crowbar and Slim Jim and neared the van. Gibson slid the tool between the window and paneling and after considerable grunt work heard the lock click open. As they lifted the handle and pulled it open, a distinctive odor escaped from the car's interior. They both knew the smell too well—the scent of death. They pulled up the bottom of their ties and placed them over their mouths. The odor carried over to the two suits, as they turned to the van at the same instant.

"Get a CSI team here ASAP," Gibson shouted.

"On the way," came an immediate response from a uniformed officer.

The SWAT team was now exiting the residence, waiting for the CSI team to sort through the apartment and gather prints, documents, and any other evidence they believed pertinent to the upcoming investigation.

Davis's voice came through the headset, commending them on their work. He then contacted the two other teams that had arrived at the locations where the two other vans had been traced to. He told them to stand off and that they had struck gold at the first site. He asked one team to drive to the site and the other to turn back around and head home. He waited for more information to be gathered from the body they had discovered.

Chapter XXIV

Rick walked the several blocks back to his car through a steady soft rain. Thunderclaps resounded in the misty late spring rain, which was a good thing in his opinion. He assumed it would disguise the sound of gunfire should the event occur this evening. And if not, he had a silencer which may have been a bit more effective. The rain was beginning to intensify, and Rick picked up his pace to a fast walk. He arrived at his car, unlocked the front door, and slid into the front seat. He brushed his hand vigorously through his hair in an attempt to dry it a bit. Reaching into the backseat, he pulled a backpack over the headrest and unzipped the front pocket. He removed a pair of dark blue nylon workout pants, a thin white stripe running down the length of the legs. He then removed a matching blue hooded pullover and laid it on the passenger seat. A pair of solid black running shoes followed, which were all necessary for added camouflage in the dark of the evening.

He removed the red Phillies T-hirt and his Levis, slipping them off past his bare feet. The tinted windows provided a dressing room obscured from any passersby. Rick pulled his workout pants up to his waistline and tied the white cord. Next he pulled the hooded shirt over his head and then took a deep breath, releasing some of his pent-up energy. He wasn't nervous but hoped his opportunity would present itself on this particular evening. He hated waiting on things that he had promised would be done. His business success was founded on this concept, and being a creature of habit, he was not about to change his MO—conveniently "forgetting" that murder used to be against his code of ethics as well.

He reached under the passenger seat and removed a box that had been taped closed. The address was bogus, as was the return address on the upper left-hand corner. He peeled off the clear tape that surrounded the box and removed its contents. It was a Ruger .357 Blackhawk, a single action six shot revolver, known as one of the most reliable weapons on the market. Also in the box was a suppressor. Rick was not gun savvy but knew what Gando had sent would be a reliable piece of equipment. Beside those were twelve rounds of ammunition in a sealed baggie. He slipped a round into each chamber and spun the barrel around for added flare. He laughed and screwed the silencer on to the long end of the handgun. He placed it under the seat and slumped back. It was now after eleven, and he had one more thing to do.

At eleven thirty Rick exited the car, his hand grasped firmly around a serrated hunting knife he had purchased at an army-navy store in Jersey. He walked the several blocks to Harrington's car. He glanced around in a 360-degree angle, noticing there was no one in sight. He crouched next to the right side front tire and plunged the knife deep into the tire's bulging exterior. A sudden blast of air escaped the inflated casing with a recognizable neoprene odor, causing the car to tilt downward to the right in a slowly descending movement. Rick withdrew the blade, slowly rose from his crouching position, and put the knife inside his front sweatshirt pocket. He headed back to his car at a normal gait and returned to the driver's seat. The pattern of the rain was still sporadic, as well as the distant distractions of thunder and lightning.

Several minutes later Rick observed the house he was studying was suddenly bathed in soft porch light. The screen door swung open and a group of three began descending the four steps on to the sidewalk. Hands were shaken, and although the voices were inaudible, it was clear the game had just broken up. Studying the group carefully, Rick noticed that Harrington was not among them. Several minutes after they dispersed two others appeared, Harrington standing on the other man's left. He was nodding as if in agreement with what had been said, and then his body gyrated in what appeared to be genuine laughter. The door then shut and the light was extinguished, indicating to Rick that the house was now void of its company. The man to Harrington's left started walking away from Rick's direction while Harrington momentarily removed a cigarette from his sports coat placed it between his lips. A flickering light appeared as the cigarette tip took on an orange hue, followed by a cone of grayish-white smoke. He placed the lighter back in his pocket and negotiated the four steps to the sidewalk.

At that instant Rick felt a surge of adrenaline along with a noticeable increase in his heart rate. The feeling was consistent with that first rush he experienced when snorting his favorite white powder. The feeling of power, strength, and invincibility was building inside him.

With his mind set on his mission, he opened his door and emerged from the car. He placed the gun inside the roomy pouch running across the length of his garment. He started a slow jogging gait, making it appear he was a neighborhood health junkie. As he approached Harrington, running alongside the cars parked on the street, he stopped and pointed to the flat tire.

"Hope that's not your car, dude," Rick muttered in his best South Philly vernacular.

"Shit, motherfucker. Yes it is, and it's starting to fucking pour. If you care to give me a hand, there's a c-note in it for you."

"Sure, pal, why not. A hundred is a hundred."

Harrington reached into his slacks and pulled out a thick, folded roll of cash. He began to peel off a hundred when he noticed his volunteer pointing a gun. Before a single word was spoken Rick squeezed the trigger three times in rapid succession, watching Harrington's limp body collapse on the damp street. With time seeming to be standing still, Rick removed the Rolex he had noticed on his victim's left wrist and took it along with the thick roll of cash that had never been returned to Harrington's pant pocket. He had planned to make it appear to be a robbery. Without panic, he placed the cash and watch into his pants pocket and trotted back to his vehicle.

The whole event took less than a minute. More importantly, Rick's actions had been automatic, as if killing a man was his daily routine. He entered the car, turned on the ignition, and drove away as if leaving a convenience store after purchasing a cup of coffee. *Smooth*, he thought.

He turned up the next side street, heading toward City Line Avenue and the ride home. A feeling of normalcy returned. Interesting was the fact that the feeling of guilt or anxiety had never entered the equation. *All in a day's work*. He slipped a disc into his player and the Talking

Heads' version of *"Psycho Killer"* emerged from the speakers. How fitting. He couldn't have chosen a more appropriate selection.

Rick turned on to the Schuylkill Expressway, starting his ride home. Before he would arrive, he would need to dispose of all items relating to his recent activities. He stayed on the route well past his exit, getting off at Interstate 95. His destination was the area along Delaware Avenue, which, of course, bordered the Delaware River. He parked at the entrance to the Moshulu, a popular gourmet restaurant and nightclub that had once been a sailing vessel. Tonight it would serve as a launching post for one gun and silencer, courtesy of Mr. Rick Grosse. He doubted if that event would ever be recorded in the ship's long and prestigious history.

After disposing of the gun, he grabbed a quick shot of brandy and went back to the spot he had parked. He drove several blocks south, stopping in front of an abandoned warehouse. He quickly changed into his original attire, balling up the incriminating outfit he'd used to commit his felony. He continued until he came to Washington Street and proceeded to drive down side streets, looking for a hungry Dumpster. Finding one, he dropped the outfit into the large green metallic container.

Getting back in the car, he slipped off the sneakers and sought out a final Dumpster to place his footwear. He passed a Police Athletic League donation bin and dropped the Nikes in for a future athlete. *How fitting,* he thought, *placing the evidence in the hands of the hunters.* He slipped on his shoes and headed back to his Center City abode. He was getting good at this, which was not something he had ever consider being proficient at or proud of doing.

At the same time, shit was going down in Brighton Beach. The CSI team had been going over the van with latex gloves, forensics photographers, and cotton swabs. But before they had even arrived at this point, bomb-sniffing dogs had been brought into the mix in order to see if any explosive materials had been planted in the van. None were found, giving way to the parade of post-crime-scene personnel.

One technician started to dust the outside of the van for fingerprints, his partner snapping photos of all examined areas. Visibly strewn inside the van were maps of Philadelphia, along with MapQuest diagrams explaining how to get there. What appeared to be a small address book was also in plain sight, along with half a dozen empty vodka bottles. No Grey Goose or Ketel One empties were visible. Did that mean crime doesn't pay?

The van was a proverbial treasure trove of evidence to be examined. Geek had worked out a deal with Captain Melitto to give Brooklyn the credit for breaking the case in return for immediate access to all crime scene materials data. They would also be copied on all information that may head to and from federal agencies. Those agencies had more manpower and better databases for dissecting incoming information. Both Davis and Eckland were masters of playing politics, their bottom line being to solve a case.

It was well past midnight when Davis signed off and left the building. There would be a plethora of information emanating from hard drives, Russian interpretation of all documents at the scene and facing the press, who were already swarming like flies. It wouldn't take a neurologist to tie the names of the city's two separate victims together, and both the *Philadelphia Daily News* and the *New York Post* would vie for the most creative and sensational headlines.

CHAPTER XVX

Rick woke the next morning, surprising himself at how calm he was from last night's extraordinary activities he'd performed. He didn't know if the killing had yet to make the morning news or tabloids, but within minutes he would check both sources.

He entered the bathroom and turned on the shower. The ringing from one of his prepaid cell phones startled him.

"Good work, kid," Gando's distinctive New York accent bellowed. "I had complete confidence in you. You came through and it means a lot, a lot for both our futures."

There was no real reason to glance at either the morning news or the headlines. The body had been found and an investigation would follow. But unlike Carl's killing, there would be absolutely *no* links to him.

"Thank you, Julian. I made a promise, and I keep my promises."

"As do I," he said. "I'll call you back in an hour with a time and place halfway between you and me. We can have lunch to settle up."

"Okay," was all Rick could muster to say. He pushed the end button and entered the shower.

———————

The Roundhouse was abuzz with high fives and nods of approval as Davis entered the lobby. He had barely slept. The pipeline of information from half a dozen law enforcement agencies began tying up many loose ends and connected many dots.

When he arrived in the third-floor conference room, most of his team was there, with high spirits and wide grins. A small stream of applause began. Even Kelley was there, against doctor's orders and still confined to a temporary wheelchair. Davis lifted his hand, and the applause slowly abated.

"I hope those cheers were for all of us. This was a team effort, and we're all responsible for bringing this case to a near end. Sit down, grab some pastries, and let's recap what we have and what we need to have, in order to send it up to the DA."

Davis began. "For starters, prints came back. Our two corpses, Petronov and Linski, deposited them all over the interior and exterior of the van we found in Brooklyn. It's obvious the three were working as a cell. The empty liquor bottles also contained prints from all three. The maps gave specific directions from Mickels' residence all the way down to point B where the murders took place. Strike two. The Feds are still going through the hard drive from the laptop, along with the address book and various papers found. Our colleagues in New York have even picked up the hookers our South Philly tough guys beat up. They admitted to having ties to our three dead guys, one of their sideline enterprises."

"Even the hookers were cleaning out some pipes. They did have an electrical and plumbing business," Hank added.

A spattering of laughter echoed in the room.

"We've got the tough guys who shot the Russians. Our ladies in New York picked them out of a lineup." Davis paused before continuing. "There are two big pieces that don't fit. First, why the bomb, and who planted it? Were the Russians shot before they could set it off, or did someone hire the Russians to seek revenge in Philly, and then blow up the whole mess? Is there a third party involved who wanted both teams out of the way? It is possible, seeing as we have no clue as to why the other Petronov was killed. I need you all to consider this angle and convince me of something.

"Here's the second problem I have. Who, if anyone, would benefit from starting a small war between these groups—and why? Do we have a third party stepping in, or did someone want to send a message? We must know these answers to close the book. Maybe some e-mails or contacts in the address book can give us some new leads. Until then, call in your informants. Ellen Sue will be coordinating evidence and leads with our Brooklyn counterparts. Fill her in on anything, no matter how trivial. I hate loose ends."

—————————

After his shower, a strange thought filled Rick's mind. Why didn't he have the balls to take action to get the woman he loved? Gando did. He could only wonder, if he had been more persistent with Brandi, what the outcome might have been. Growing up, his parents had taken a very hands-off approach toward his development. On several occasions, when he had been suspended from school for inane actions, he was never punished or lectured. His father would tell him that right or wrong, only he could correct his mistakes: *No one should or could tell you what to do. You must learn for yourself, both through good, thought-out actions, and those that are harmful to yourself or others. Forcing you to do something would only make you more resentful and disobedient. Life has many lessons,* his father would say. *Do whatever it takes to make that journey comfortable and rewarding. When you start to doubt your actions, something is wrong.*

The phone rang, interrupting his self-analysis. Gando spoke. "Rick, get off exit 10 on the New Jersey Turnpike. Meet me at the Skylark Diner for lunch, on route 1 south."

Rick's reply was rapid: "See you then."

The phone line went dead.

Rick figured it would take about an hour and change to make the drive to New Brunswick. Rick knew a business associate in New Brunswick and might stop off to visit on the way home. Before leaving, he picked up one of his temporary cell phones and called Abbey. After two rings, the phone went to voice mail. He left a message saying he wanted to see her later that evening, if she was not entertaining, and treat her to dinner. Neither of them had been questioned further about Carl's murder. He stuffed his wallet in the front pocked of his jeans and proceeded to get his car.

The drive up the turnpike was mundane at best. The scenery consisted of large, high tension wires, empty warehouses for lease, and billboards advertising everything from cars to concerts to lawyers who could make a DUI go away. He listened to WIP, the Philly sports station, and all the negative criticism the Phillies were getting after losing three straight.

Before no time, the sign for his exit appeared on the horizon, *Exit 10, and keep right*. He downshifted at the curve to the tolls, slowing down with ticket in hand. Although the EZ Pass system, which deducted tolls from a credit account, was easier, he hated having any records of his whereabouts. He slowed to a stop and paid the toll, smiling at the cute toll collector and wishing her a nice day. Who could have a nice day breathing in nasty fumes, standing in a small booth, and holding her arm out the window all day long? Knowing the average salary for that position averaged sixty-five thousand, probably a lot of people!

He veered to the right after the exit, entering Route 1 north. Several miles later, he made a U-turn, or jug handle as the sign read, passing the diner on the left. Most major New Jersey suburban roads are divided by concrete barriers, sometimes requiring one to drive several miles before they can turn around. Perhaps the reason Jersey natives were often frustrated drivers.

He made the turn and pulled into the crowded parking lot. He left the car and approached the entrance (two large stainless steel windowed doors topped by a red and white six-sided roof).

He saw Gando waiving from a booth on the left. The décor was art deco at its finest, the interior decorated by multicolored tiled columns. Rick slid into the blue vinyl booth directly across from Gando. They nodded at each other and extended their hands.

"Pleasure to see you, Rick," Julian said.

"Likewise," Rick responded.

"You are a very prompt and reliable individual. Those are two traits I tend to admire in a man."

"Thanks, Julian. It's the way I was brought up. I was taught to respect people as long as they respect me," he said. Just then, the server approached with two glossy covered menus, as well as a pot of hot coffee. Rick ordered the coffee and Julian an iced tea with lemon.

"Look at the menu, and I'll be back in a minute, hon," the waitress uttered as she glance at Julian. Rick smiled.

The two men perused the menu consisting of salads, breakfast dishes, and an eclectic mix of choices covering Asian and European dishes.

The waitress approached, pencil in hand, and said with a drone, "You gentlemen know what you's having?"

Rick ordered a cup of lobster bisque and a Cuban burger. Julian opted for the French onion soup and a shrimp Caesar salad with the garlic grilled shrimp. It was a healthy choice, accompanied by his obligatory Italian touch. They folded their menus and returned them to the server's outstretched hand. She thanked them and promised to return shortly.

Julian's hand reached down to the area on his right and returned with a rectangular box wrapped in a plain, dark blue paper.

"Hey kid, this is for you," he whispered. "There are a hundred large in here. We still owe you four, which will follow as soon as the insurance money is released. The case was called a robbery, and there are no suspicious circumstances saying anything else. Just make sure that the Rolex and anything else you took will never be tied back to you."

"Taken care of Julian," Rick replied. "Glad I could help you out, and you have been more than generous with my fee."

The waitress appeared, soups in hand, and placed the correct item down in front of the pair. As they ate, they filled the other in on their past two weeks since they had last met. Julian was busy cleaning up some small turf problems between two disputing families.

"Nothing terribly problematic. A simple conflict of interest. I have interests, and they conflict with them." He also mentioned that he would lay low with Bryant for the time being, not wanting to attract any unwanted attention to either of them.

Rick mentioned that Abbey had talked him into taking scuba lessons. She had grown up on the Jersey Shore. Her summers were spent on Long Beach Island, where she loved the ocean. Some of her friends took up surfing, but she chose diving, which she still loved to this day. Conversations continued throughout lunch, with their respective home team fanaticism about the Phillies and the Yankees.

Even as they spoke, Rick kept the box close to his side, guarding the large sum of money, his motivation for his past action.

No dessert was ordered, and as the check arrived, Julian's cat-like motion snared the check as it left its black vinyl housing. "This is on me, end of story," he barked.

Rick nodded and smiled in appreciation, mentioning that it was his turn next time. The two men rose, clutched in the obligatory "Godfather hug," and left the building. They would be strangers for a time to come, or at least until some poor schmuck was hauled in for Harrington's murder. Life was good.

Rick had not yet heard from Abbey about this evening, so he texted her to let him know whether he could treat her to a night on the town. He aimed the car down Route 1 south, exiting at Rutgers University. He was visiting Tommy O'Shea, another high school buddy he still was in contact with. Tommy had worked for the Philadelphia Parking Authority. At that time, they were just a bunch of ticket writers, getting cursed, threatened, and insulted for just doing their jobs. With the advent and popularity of reality shows, the PPA is now a more glamorous occupation, being local stars and noticing an abatement of abuse their predecessors had endured.

Rick had loaned Tommy five grand to get his new business started. Tommy bought an old delivery van and converted it into a restaurant on wheels. It was called **Man Bites Dog** and was a popular dining spot on campus. Besides, Tommy had a continuous flow of extra-curricular revenue from the attractive young co-eds.

Rick approached and tapped the window. Tommy turned, and a big ear-to-ear grin appeared on his round face. "Yo, Rick. Yo, man. You didn't drive up here for one of my gourmet meals, did you?" he cajoled.

"Nah, just wanted to see your ugly face," he said.

Rick's loan helped Tommy get started, as well as save him the usury interest charged by loan sharks. He would have to pay Rick back a sum of $500 per month for one full year. This would cover the original five thousand, as well as 20 percent interest for the term. This was a far cry from the 5 to 10 percent per week, which was the going street rate. He always paid on time and never complained.

"You did an awesome job on the truck," Rick said. "I remember when it was a pure white shell with a stinking odor."

"Thanks, dude," Tommy said with pride.

Tommy told Rick to give him three minutes. In that time, he quickly assembled two gourmet meals in appreciation to his pal. All of his selections were named after breeds of dog. The first was the French Poodle, containing melted Boursin, capers, and a light béchamel sauce, inserted into a fresh croissant. The second was the Chihuahua, an all-beef dog topped with taco meat, tomatoes, salsa, habanera peppers, and cheddar cheese. No Tums were included. Rick smiled, informing Tommy he had just finished lunch.

"No problema, man. I'll wrap them in foil and you can take them home."

Rick took the brown bag containing the heartburn and bid him farewell.

He walked back to the car, checked his message-less phone, and headed back down the turnpike to his city of birth. He didn't know yet, but it was the beginning of an even more dangerous path he would take.

PART THREE

Chapter XXVI

As the Fourth of July loomed several days away, the Roundhouse was readying up for a wedding on the upcoming weekend. Things had been good for the team of OCTF members. For one, Kelley's recovery was way ahead of schedule. Fewer than two months earlier the group had been more prepared for a funeral than a joyous wedding celebration. Kelley had surprised them and proved them all wrong. He jokingly mentioned that the only thing he would request at the party would be his future wife not consume any of the wedding cake. Ashley was the only one who laughed, promising to provide some feminine Viagra just in case.

The case in Brooklyn had been pretty much cleared up as the gun found at the crime scene yielded an arrest. The gun had been sent to the ATF in Washington DC for closer scrutiny. Using the Magnaflux method, the scientist magnetizes the firearm, which produces ripples of magnetic force. It is then sprayed with oil that suspends iron-like particles that settle into the area, producing a readable format. That was the easy part. The gun had been sold at a gun show in Central Pennsylvania to an arms dealer in Brooklyn. After threatening the owner with a variety of violations, he produced the sales slip, which led to the arrest. Paulie "the Piece" Petiole was taken into custody. Curiously though, his name "the piece" did not originate from his gun collection but from the bad hairpiece he awkwardly wore. The cops couldn't tie Paulie to the victim, so they figured it had been a contract hit. Paulie was old school, took the fall, and plea-bargained it down to eight-and-a-half to fifteen years for third-degree murder. They may never know the reason for the hit, but the dead Russian and Paulie yielded two more bad guys out of circulation. Both were from distinctly separate criminal families, families who were now in such a state of utter disarray the "crime" could be dropped from their description.

The investigation into the robbery/homicide in May of Harrington Alexander Marcus III near City Line Avenue remained unsolved. Of the several witnesses interviewed, descriptions of the perpetrator ranged from two white teenagers in gray hoodies to a tanned Mexican with short-cropped black hair. The leads went nowhere, and the case was slowly easing into the cold case files. Montgomery County does not have many homicides, and the media's criticism of the poor investigation and lack of evidence quickly died down within several days of the incident. No more robberies occurred as patrols were stepped up and more, brighter street lights were installed within several of the upper class neighborhoods.

The case of Carl Mickels may have cooled off, but it was not at all gone. Everywhere Davis turned he seemed to find a link back to the prime suspect, Rick Grosse. His wits were stretched to such a degree he was beginning to think the hookers hired for the Jersey party-goers were products of Grosse's *Full Service Concierges*. It was well known already the girls worked for Abbey Roads, Grosse's alibi in the Carl murder.

But maybe Davis was just being paranoid.

Rick passed his time having fun. The "new" Rick was trying to create outlets to replace his evil ways. He attended several Phillies home games during the month, as they maintained a five game divisional lead as the All Star break neared. He even took the two-hour ride up the turnpike to catch them visiting the New York Mets at their new ballpark, City Field, in Queens, New York. They batted around in the fourth and trounced the Mets 11–2.

He also attended weekly scuba diving classes at an old established diving store that gave out certifications upon completion of the curriculum. He enjoyed it, a steady passion for it growing inside him. He thanked Abbey each and every time they spoke. To thank her, he booked a seven-day Carnival cruise in the Caribbean, which even included a port of call in St. Maartin. He assumed it would be a bit safer these days, knowing the outcome of Esperanza's recent fate.

They left a week after the Mainline murder, flying down to Miami a night prior to the ship's departure, and partied all night at South Beach. Rick had brought down his obligatory stash of cocaine and pills, adding to his euphoria, while clubbing at The Roof, the SkyBar, and Amnesia, some of the chic nightspots in town. When the cache of party goods was nearing completion, they arrived at their hotel just before 6:00 a.m., leaving fewer than two hours to recover and arrive at the embarkation site. With reddened eyes and dry mouths, they kicked into fourth gear, arriving with little time to spare.

The large ship blew its horn, leaving the Miami skyline behind in what seemed like minutes. They clinked their complimentary glasses of champagne, spilling most of it on the deck. They decided to head back to their ocean view deluxe stateroom in order to fully recover for the days ahead. They wearily approached the elevator to the spacious suites. As they entered the room, they quickly peeled off their outerwear and collapsed on the king-sized bed. Their relationship combined friendship, business, past experiences, and sex. They were good friends, with the proverbial benefits included. They faced each other, rolling onto their sides in a skin on skin embrace. At that moment, a loud, static-filled authoritative voice came over the ship's loudspeakers.

"*The emergency signal will be sounded. It will consist of seven short blasts followed by one long blast on the ship's whistle.*"

A loud shrill noise filled their peaceful surroundings.

"*This drill is required by international law, and all passengers must attend wearing a life jacket, whether you have cruised with us or not. Safety information and instructions are posted in the stateroom. If you are traveling with small children, please contact the stateroom attendant, and a life jacket will be issued for them. All guests will be assembled for a roll call, and all activities suspended during the drill. This is last call for all guests not sailing with us to exit the vessel. The drill will begin in fifteen minutes. Thank you all in advance for your cooperation and for choosing Carnival Cruise Lines.*"

They both laughed. They would have to wait for what seemed like an eternity for the real vacation to start.

The next several days were filled with blue skies, smooth waters, and a hedonistic lifestyle. They closed the clubs on several nights, as well as donated several thousand at the small onboard casino. They dined on oysters Rockefeller, fresh stone crab claws, twenty-ounce rib eyes, and baked Alaska.

On the fourth day they took a jitney into Phillipsburg (at one time the capital of the Dutch-owned half of the island) and rented a car for the day. Rick drove her around, playing tour guide while making several stops at his former favorite haunts. They stopped at the Boathouse in Simpson Bay, as Rick had been craving a bowl of his favorite conch chowder. She loved it too. They next headed over to Marigot, shopping at the designer stores and the open air market that sold clothing, spices, and jewelry all indigenous to the area. At the outdoor market, a small display table containing turquoise-like jewelry caught her attention. She waited for one of the attractive English accented owners to acknowledge her. The prices were extremely reasonable and Rick told her to pick out several she liked. Two hundred and eighty dollars later she left with a uniquely modeled bracelet, matching earrings, and a necklace that Rick had admired. She gave Rick a playful kiss and thanked him. He smiled and muttered that she was welcome. They had time for a light snack before they were due back at the jitney.

They walked over to the outdoor café area surrounding the inlet and entered an open air French Patisserie. It was an awesome meal in an awesome, picturesque surrounding. They paid the bill, Abbey insisting it was her treat, and they headed back to the jitney. Rick enjoyed the excursion, but something wasn't perfect. Abbey wasn't quite tall enough, her face not heart-shaped enough, her hair too unnatural … basically, she wasn't what Rick was hoping she would be—he was hoping she would be another person.

The final few days were spent lounging on the deck, staring out at the tranquil, aqua-blue waters. They also tried their hands at skeet shooting, slamming golf balls into the depths of the ocean, and half a day at the adult-only Serenity retreat. They took advantage of a deep-tissue message, impeccable service, and playing footsies in the whirlpool. Rick commented the name fit the experience.

As the ship pulled into the port of Miami, they agreed they'd had an incredible week at sea. They waited in line to exit the vessel, the line moving slowly due to thank-yous offered by the staff. Their luggage appeared without any delays and they grabbed a cab to the airport.

The lines at the TSA's checkpoints were small and moved at light speed compared to Philadelphia.

Abbey picked up a *Cosmopolitan* to read on the plane, and Rick grabbed a *Sports Illustrated*. As Rick went to pay, he was amused at the bold print on the right side of the magazine's border. It read, *"Fifty-six things a man loves to be woken up to in the morning."*

He nudged Abbey and pointed to the title, saying, "Damn, Abbey, and I thought there was only one thing."

She smiled as the loudspeaker asked all first-class passengers to board the 777. In fewer than three hours the plane gently touched down in his favorite city. They collected their luggage, rode up two floors in the elevator, and retrieved his car. He dropped her off at her residence, kissed her lips in a nonseductive manner, and told her what a great time he'd had. She thanked him, her index finger tapping the newly appearing bulge inside his pants, and asked if he would like to spend the night. He politely declined and said they should get together later in the week. Their relationship had no expectations, requirements, or demands. *It doesn't get much better than this,* Rick thought.

He drove the ten minutes back to his place. He parked, went upstairs, and threw his luggage in the living room. It could wait till tomorrow. He entered his bedroom, removed his clothes, and was asleep in a heartbeat.

CHAPTER XXVII

If it had been a day later, Jimmy and Caitlin would not have had a June wedding. They had planned a simple ceremony, held in downtown Philadelphia at a small historic church. Along with the team from the OCTF, several dozen friends and family were in attendance. Caitlin wore her mother's wedding dress, which had been saved for this very occasion (hoping it would be sooner than later). She'd had it tailored in hopes of a somewhat more vogue fashion look. Nothing was worse than shoulder pads and fifty-year-old lace with a small Queen of Rochester hat planted on her head. Jimmy donned a black Armani tuxedo (rented) at his future bride's insistence. The actual service was short, each reciting his and her own memorized vows, promises of a life full of happiness and memories that would remain everlasting were shared. After the ceremonial "I dos," they kissed and embraced in a passionate display, drawing oohs and aahs from the gallery. They were young, middle class, and in love. It was the love story of the twenty-first century, with tight budgets, close family, and the occasional bombing mishap all thrown into the mix. Applause followed the nuptials and they were off to celebrate the special evening that would mark a future of wedded bliss.

What was left of ceremonial expenses (such as the league of thirty-eight bridesmaids and enough flowers to cause a worldwide anaphylactic attack) was made up for at the reception. Romance came in the form of the Spirit of Philadelphia, a local cruise ship docked under the shadows of the Ben Franklin Bridge. Several loud blasts emanated from the ship's horn, marking the union of the couple, as well as the start of the night's festivities. The crowd was ushered into the reception area, with Jimmy and Caitlin bursting into the packed room like the stars of a red-carpet event. Cocktails and appetizers were served and the party began. The almost full moon glistened off the ship's starboard bow, adding an extra romantic flair to the ambiance.

"The moon came extra," Jimmy said. "I knew a guy who knew a guy, who knew *another* guy, who knew how to push back a wedding date in a creative way."

Throughout the evening, guests recounted stories of the couple's past, with laughter and alcohol flowing freely. The more the alcohol flowed, the more embarrassing the stories became. Jimmy knew he was lucky to be standing there, the ugly memories of his near-death experience never fully leaving his thoughts, the fresh scars on his face harsh reminders. Everyone there knew that as well, making the party even more special.

Davis offered the toast, wishing them both future successes. As the ship headed back to port, the party was still in high gear and ready to continue the celebration until kingdom come.

As they disembarked the ship, several limousines were in line waiting to bring anyone who was willing (and still standing) over to the Sugarhouse Casino only a few blocks away. The cars were quickly populated with guests, the seating area loaded with chilled champagne, and they were off on the five-minute ride.

Arriving at the entrance, they were escorted in by several enormous men in suits. One "party-too-harder" mistook the bouncers for an Eagles lineman and was dead set on swindling an autograph out of him. The VIP treatment was evident as they were escorted to a waiting, empty blackjack table. The team sat down to play, taking out new twenties recently obtained from the numerous cash machines. The casino treated the wedding clan like gold.

"Make sure Caitlin is holding those envelopes. You don't want to piss her off this quick," Davis joked.

"I'll be lucky if see any of it," Jimmy replied, struggling to keep himself seated on his high-backed chair.

Struggling to add the card totals, Geek helped out with numbers as he always did. The table went on a run, watching the dealer pass 21 on what seemed like ten straight hands. Loud laughter and high fives circled the table as the pile of chips grew in front of each gambler. The table volume lowered slightly as the house inexorably began to recoup some of its losses.

"Time to hit the head," Davis said in a slightly slurred mumble. He rose from his chair, feeling the effects of his intoxication, but knew he had a mission to empty his overflowing bladder. A passing cocktail waitress pointed to the restroom as if reading Davis's mind. He nodded to thank her and headed toward it. Gibson caught up with him, needing to relieve himself too, as well as make sure the boss was okay.

Just then, a man walking at a quick pace bumped shoulders with Davis, knocking him off balance. As he lifted his head, his eyes met with the man's. It was Rick Grosse.

"Out of all the gin joints in all the world, you had to walk into mine," Davis snapped.

Grosse was ready to push the guy away, stopping when he noticed who it was. "Well if it's not Philadelphia's finest! I sure hope you're off the clock," Grosse uttered sarcastically. His smile was cocky, as always. It was obvious his head was clearer then Davis's.

Seeing what was about to transpire, Gibson grabbed Davis's shoulder, and turning to Grosse, said, "This is not the time or place. Keep walking or I'll make a call and you can spend the night at *our* house."

Grosse held back, picking up the pace in the opposite direction.

This encounter had sobered Davis up fast.

Gibson told him to forget about it, that it wasn't worth ruining a good evening over. "We can pay him a visit soon. We both know that prick is guilty and we'll eventually prove it. There is a time and place for everything, and this isn't that time."

They continued to the bathroom, Davis regaining his composure along the way. But Gibson was right. They could pay Grosse a visit. Even if they did, what good would it do? What new evidence did they have? Could they tie Rick to the Jersey hookers through Abbey? Probably not; it was a theory at best and a thready one at that. Davis tried to forget the encounter. It wasn't fair for Jimmy or Caitlin to dwell on it now.

Rick headed toward the exit, stunned by the chance encounter. He hadn't heard from the cops in several months and was slightly cocky that he may no longer be a person of interest. Hopefully this reunion would not bring him back into the limelight.

He stepped into the humid summer night, handed his ticket to the valet, and waited for his ride. He slipped the valet a ten, slid into the seat, and drove home, a little less secure than he wanted to be. He didn't get ten minutes up the road before his nerves forced him to pull over. In seconds he was out of the driver seat. Rick pulled out his little black device and ran it all around his car. It told him that indeed his car was still bug-free. So much for top police work! By now, he figured the cops would have at least put six tracking devices in his car, half a dozen listening bugs, and maybe just a handful of cameras. But his personal fuzz-buster told him he was clean. A little more at ease, he headed back to his driver's seat.

CHAPTER XXVIII

Over the course of the next several weeks, Rick's anxiety began to subside. His literal run-in with the law at the casino had unnerved him. His cockiness morphed into paranoia that he would again be questioned by the authorities in regard to Carl's homicide. During that time he laid low, increased his scuba lessons, dined out locally, and distanced himself from his past connections. The uncomfortable heat wave that plagued Philadelphia also added to his self-inflicted hibernation. He spent time with Abbey on occasion, feeling the sexual and emotional need for a woman's company. She filled both of those needs, but not in a romantic sense. Only Brandi had all that, and he wondered if anyone else could ever compare. As far as *Full Service Concierges* went … it couldn't. The venture was officially dead on the street. Rick couldn't stick his neck out and take any unnecessary risks while the law was still on him.

His phone rang. It was the one connecting him to Bryant. "Bryant, it's so nice to hear from you. How has life been treating you lately?"

"Hi, Rick. It's been so much better without Harrington," she replied, with no hesitation or doubt in her voice.

"I haven't spoken to Julian in ages. How has he been?" Rick asked with an obvious sincerity.

"We keep in touch, but I'm waiting for the smoke to clear from this whole tragedy. Some investigators from both the police and insurance company have spoken with me. They said they needed information. Things like if he had any enemies, owed people money, and the like. I really believe they're following the robbery gone bad route. It's a shame in a way that the justice system can be so easily duped. Makes you think about life."

Both Rick and Bryant knew it would be stupid to see Gando until the insurance investigation had been wrapped up.

Bryant continued. "I have a proposition for you, Rick."

"It seems I've heard that same line from you in the past," he replied, "From another close friend of ours."

She paused, reassuring him that it was not another dirty job to do. "On the contrary," she said, recognizing his concern and curiosity, "I work out several days a week at a nearby gym. Every Tuesday and Saturday I attend a spin class with a friend I met there several months ago. Her name is Adrianna, and she's a looker as well as a sweetheart."

Rick began to interrupt, but she told him to let her finish.

"She's originally from Philadelphia but is quite well traveled. She is well educated and has a nice job in upper management with Comcast."

"Okay, Bryant, where's the catch?" He tried to remember where he'd heard the name before. Didn't Gando mention a friend named Adrianna?

"She's in a similar position as I'd been prior to becoming a widow. In our post-workout breakfasts, she's mentioned that she's sort of in the market for a friend with benefits."

"Go on," Rick added, his voice denoting a hint of carnal interest.

"Her husband is a high-powered financial attorney, his firm being on a retainer with several large banks. He's away from home more than he's there. Adrianna is entering the prime of her sexual awareness, and the bottom line is, her hubby just ain't getting it done for her. Follow my drift?"

Rick was following it and repeated the question, "Where's the catch?"

"I thought in my limited matchmaking experience, knowing the two of you, you just might be a good fit and hit it off."

Rick processed the proposition. "Hell, why not?" he answered with the obvious male curiosity. "Okay. So she's smart and well traveled. Give me a rundown on features, height and the rest."

"I guess she's about five feet five inches, with dark eyes, high cheekbones, and a straight nose. She's in really good shape, slightly above average breasts, and carries herself extremely well. As I said, she's a looker."

Rick pondered the proposition for less than a second. "Bryant, give me her number, as I assume you have already told her I was interested."

Bryant smiled, slightly impressed with Rick's intuition about girl talk, and she gave him the number. "Call her soon. Her husband will be out of town for at least another few days. As you men say, the ball is in your court."

"Bryant, thanks."

"And by the way, we should have your balance on the way within the next month. 'Bye, sweetie!"

The connection went silent and Rick closed the cell. He was actually looking forward to this new woman. After all, she was married, and this meant that it could turn out to be a fun time for all, without the hassle of commitment.

No sooner had Rick ended his conversation with Bryant, his main cell phone rang. The number and ID that flashed across the screen indicated a familiar number: the OCTF. He let it ring three times, deciding to meet the call head-on rather than letting it go to his voice mail.

"Yo, Rick here."

"Mr. Grosse?" Davis chided. "Davis here; remember me? We ran into each other at the casino, and we never finished our short talk."

"What can I do for you, Davis?"

"Well, for starters—if it's convenient of course—there are still some questions I'd like to ask you regarding Carl's murder. We'd like to finally eliminate you as a person of interest."

"I thought you already had," Rick replied.

"Loose ends, you know. How would two o'clock be? You know where my office is."

"Two is fine, but I do have plans for the evening. Can you promise to get me out of there by, say, two thirty?"

"I'll do my best. See you in an hour then. Thank you," was the final reply before the line went dead.

Rick sat down in his recliner, lit a cigarette, and took a long, slow drag. He blew the smoke out in small rings, followed by a long stream as he pondered which questions Davis might ask. He assumed if any hard evidence existed, Rick would have already been in custody and charged. Davis would show photos of the crime scene, studying Rick's reactions to the most vivid pictures. He would then ask for his alibi, hoping he would trip him up and get a different story than Rick had given him during the first interview. Rick knew Davis was smart, so he had to be smarter. What helped was his believing he *was* smarter.

He finished his smoke, popped a Xanax (knowing that would keep his emotions under control), and got dressed. He decided not to call his lawyer, thinking such an action might lead Davis into thinking he had something to hide.

He zipped up his jeans, grabbed the car keys, and headed downtown. As he drove, he punched Adrianna's number into his phone's contact list. He would call on the way home, seeing if she were available to meet him later. He knew that when women were called so quickly after giving out a phone number, some think the guy is hard up or desperate. Rick was neither. He just wanted to explore this new avenue that Bryant had given him. *Nothing ventured, nothing gained,* he surmised, pulling into a parking lot across the street from the Roundhouse.

Rick parked the car and crossed the street, entering at the main vestibule. He passed groups of uniformed and plainclothes officers, recognizing several. He had some friends in the department, but acknowledging them in public was not the right thing to do for their cover or his own.

He approached the large, circular information desk in the lobby and said to the attractive brunette working the station, "I have a meeting with Stephen Davis. Can you call his office and tell him Rick Grosse is here?"

She picked up the phone and ran her finger down a white sheet of paper filled with names and numbers. She located his extension and pressed the digits into the phone's keypad. Seconds later she returned the receiver to the cradle, grabbed a sticky note, and wrote down the room number. She then handed him a visitor's pass, mentioning to wear it around his neck while in the building and then return it before his exit. Pointing to the bank of elevators, the receptionist then returned to answering a call that had come in.

Rick entered the elevator, pressed 3, and took the quick ride to

Davis's floor. He exited the elevator and noticed a small sign, pointing him in the right direction. He passed several banks of cubicles, occupied by serious-looking men and women, some scribbling notes on pads and others cradling the phone on their shoulders and chatting away. He approached the office coinciding to the numbers written on the note and knocked. Several seconds later, the door swung open, as Davis acknowledged his visitor.

"Please come in, Mr. Grosse. Take the seat over there." Davis indicated a wooden chair with chipping armrests. "Thank you for coming in on such short notice, Mr. Grosse," Davis uttered in a controlled manner.

"My pleasure," Rick countered. "Now what was it you wanted to talk to me about?"

Davis picked up a manila folder from a small stack that occupied a portion of his desk. He opened it, removing several up-close–and-personal photos of Carl. One depicted his pale white face, partially buried under the debris that had hidden his body. A second photo revealed Carl's body sprawled out on an autopsy table, showing distorted limbs, cuts, and bruises, that had been the result of a building collapsing on a two-hundred pound body. The third pictured two dead bodies occupying the sidewalk in front of the south Philadelphia Social Club bombings. Davis glanced up at Rick, noticing no reaction other than interest in the photo.

"The first two are of your partner—or should I say ex-partner. We know what you guys did. We'd been building a case, and a damn good one, against the both of you, until this tragedy occurred. What can you tell me about it?"

"Tell you about what?" Rick replied in an almost naïve fashion.

"Did you know that Carl had been working with us? We had him nailed, and he squawked. He was rolling on you, and your little business was finished. Then we would tackle you on some of your connections, right down the line, cleaning all the dirt and scum off the streets of this city." His tone was escalating in both passion and intensity.

"Detective Davis," Rick began. "Agreed, we are not choir boys but at the same time not hardened criminals or thugs. We were both just trying to make a living. We cut corners here and there, but we were not killers. We had both spent time locked up and swore to each other it would not happen again. Off the record, you have nothing on us, or we would have been locked up a while ago. Carl is dead and I had *zilch* to do with that horrific act," Rick stated. "Some of the people we got involved with were ruthless, and yes we did piss some people off. But shit, we never crossed that line. Go find his killer, and I'll help you all I can to convict the son of a bitch."

Rick was at the top of his game and enjoyed watching Davis's reaction. He gauged that his soliloquy had been stellar, worthy of at least an Oscar nomination. Davis did not move or interrupt him as he gave his speech.

"As for those two stiffs lying on the sidewalk, I had seen a similar photo in the *Daily News*. Not as graphic, but similar."

"I was just curious to get your take on it. One of our men was severely injured, but thank God he made a full recovery. We think, or at least our fellow officers in Brooklyn do, that we solved the case, but if you can offer any insight, your help will be duly noted."

During the next twenty minutes or so, they discussed the state of organized crime within the city. Neither of them fully laid their cards on the table, but both expressed concern and pride in making their city the best in America. Davis was not totally convinced of Rick's involvement in the murder, although Rick was convinced that he quashed, or at least eased, Davis's obsession with solving the case.

Rick stood up. "If I can be of any further assistance, please do not hesitate to get in touch," Rick spouted. He was spreading his manure like a mushroom farmer in Kennet Square.

"I appreciate your coming in on such short notice," Davis added. He played the part as if he was convinced, knowing that sort of reassurance was exactly what Rick needed.

Rick offered his hand and Davis shook, thanking him again and wishing him a pleasant day. Once the room was vacant, Davis waved a hand at the one camera he knew was closest.

In an adjoining office, Geek and Ellen Sue were watching the live performance as video cameras taped the interview. They would analyze speech, body language, and the facts of the case in order to draw any conclusions. The cameras were well hidden, and even if Rick had suspected them he did nothing to change his performance. They watched Rick leave the room, and Davis took his seat.

The door of Davis's office swung open, Ellen Sue and the Geek filing in.

"It's great to be Catholic and go to confession. You could start over every week," Davis spouted, ever quoting *A Bronx Tale.* "Grosse walked out of this office thinking that he was free and clear. He also left believing he would be doing us a great service by staying in touch with us, as well as keeping us informed about what was happening on the street, that we would treat him special for giving us information. He thinks he's starting over."

The pair looked at each other, not only because of Davis's overused redundant quotes, but because he was right. At the same time Rick was giving the interview, one of Geek's men was installing a high frequency tracking device that was detectable only with the most modern bug detectors. It was a model that was in the testing phases. Although its reliability was not 100 percent accurate, it was pretty close, and they could keep tabs on Rick without him suspecting a thing. They had also planted a device that was easily detectable, assuming once he found it, he would believe he was free and clear and that everything had been successfully removed.

Rick approached the elevator, hiding all of his emotions and cockiness, stemming from the belief that he had successfully sold Davis a bill of goods. Rick left the building and walked at a steady gait toward his car.

Rick navigated up the Expressway the fifteen minute ride home. The city was empty this evening, as it usually was during the summer months. The city's inhabitants tend to migrate to the Jersey and Delaware shores, trading the city's concrete for the sand and surf of the Atlantic Ocean.

As Rick pulled up to his building, he grabbed his phone, which had stored Adrianna's number. He located the bookmark on his favorites list and pressed send. He anxiously awaited, hoping the call was not routed to her voice mail. Seconds later the voice mail picked up, telling her callers that she would be home around five and to leave a message or to call her back then. There was something in her voice that immediately grabbed Rick's attention, stirring up something in his memory. Although Bryant had said that she was originally from Philly, there was little hint of any accent or familiarity. He punched the end button, deciding to try again after five. He could try to solve what had pushed an unfamiliar button within his mind by then.

He entered his place, customarily locking the door behind him. He emptied his pockets on the side table, letting its contents spill over the glass surface. That was when a peculiar light caught his attention. After a few moments of total confusion, the realization hit home. The light was from his fuzz-buster. The clever little devise changed LED lights to indicate the presence of a listening or tracking signal. Currently it was indicating both.

Rick smiled. *Cops*, he thought, *trying to be all smart and cute with me*. He picked up the device and ran it along the table until it picked up a closer signal. He leaned down, pulled out the table's single drawer, and removed the green circuit board disk attached to its bottom. *Clever*, he thought, *but ultimately pointless*.

Chapter XXIX

It was slightly after three in the afternoon on Friday. Davis sat alone in his office. He needed to further process Rick's demeanor and go over the taping of the interview with a behavioral analyst. There would be time for that. He headed toward the bank of elevators, and with a brisk pace toward his car and his bimonthly ritual, which always saddened him.

He first drove the dozen blocks toward Chinatown, pulling up in front of his favorite eatery. Not even opening the menu, he placed his usual order and sat down for the brief wait. With lightning speed he received the take out order, paid, and continued on his short excursion.

He weaved his way through the early rush hour traffic, which was unusually light for that time of day. Twenty minutes later he pulled up to a line of nondescript row homes that were synonymous with middle-class Philadelphia. He climbed up a low angled ramp rather than using the five steps. His brother was already out on the porch, smiling as his older sibling arrived.

"You're late as unusual, brother," Michael said, smiling with his patented ear-to-ear grin. "Least you didn't cancel. I know I'm a boring slacker, but God, man, a little brotherly love goes a long way."

"I got held up a little past my schedule, interviewing one of the bad guys," he responded, leaning down to hug his younger brother. His wheelchair was at least a modern version, allowing his body to be propped up almost eye level. Some said it was a self-esteem boost for the physically inept. Others thought it was just like having the latest model of Porsche on the market. Michael was a blend of both these ideals.

Michael was seven years Davis's junior. On his eighteenth birthday, he'd enlisted to serve his country. After training at Fort Dix in an infantry as a communications specialist, he was shipped out to fight in the Persian Gulf. His unit served near the front lines, gathering and deciphering intelligence and then sending it back to the military strategists, who then planned future tactical strikes. The Iraqis had planted thousands of landmines, both antipersonnel and antitank types, the latter being much more potent.

On a routine scouting mission Michael's unit stumbled upon a so-called "safe passage area," which turned out to be quite the opposite. Several trucks believed to be free of danger set off several of these massively fatal devices. Michael had been walking on the truck's flank when one device was set off. The explosion hurled a barrage of shrapnel and jagged metal shards with lightning-fast force in a multitude of directions. One piece of metal tore through his protective vest, slicing into his spine.

His next recollection was of lying in a bed in a mobile hospital and having no sensation below his waist. He was alive, but was paralyzed from the waist down. Other members of the crew were not as lucky, as a dozen of his buddies lost their lives. He was discharged and awarded several medals, and after months of rehab was given a generous pension, a group house to live in with fellow soldiers, and transported back to his home town of Philadelphia.

During his rehab, the government also trained him in computer skills, using him on a consultant basis for special projects. He had an affinity for the growing use of computers in the dotcom era and was very talented when it came to "hacking," at that time a newly budding endeavor. His services were used by Homeland Security, the FBI, and even the OCTF on some occasions. It gave him a sense of patriotic duty as well as some extra income. These series of events were one of the reasons his older brother had joined up with the task force to begin with. Both Davis boys were joining in doing their part for the US of A.

Stephen handed over a yellow bag from his brother's favorite Chinatown restaurant. Michael pulled out a clear, one-quart container of roast pork noodle soup. It was followed by a white Styrofoam box containing his favorite fried wontons. His captivating smile reappeared.

"Thanks, bro." Michael beamed.

"Not a problem, hero," was the lighthearted and sincere response.

They shared stories to catch up since their last visit, sporadic laughter filling the space surrounding them. Andre Romero, one of his housemates and buddies from his unit, appeared carrying two Rolling Rocks. He thrust one in each of the brother's directions, shook Stephen's outstretched hand, and returned back to the house.

"I might have some work for you, bro. My investigation into that bombing case I told you about is hurdling to the cold case basement, and I know this guy is guilty as shit."

Stephen scribbled a name and address down on a scrap of paper and handed it to his brother. "If you get a chance, see if you can put your talents to a good use for me. Break into his computer and let me know if you see any type of incriminating evidence or something that looks out of the ordinary. Focus on bank transactions, searches made and erased, and anything you find suspicious. Keep this between us girls, if you know what I mean."

"You know you can't use what I find. Not if you're going to charge the guy." Michael pointed out.

"I just need a lead. Not the evidence to sink him with. Do what you can."

Michael folded the slip and inserted it into a pouch that was hanging off the side of his wheelchair. He nodded and mentioned he would treat it as code red. They both laughed.

Stephen continued to fill his brother in on the case. Several years ago, his brother had sent a Trojan virus into the computer of a suspected terrorist cell operating in the proximity of the White House. This gave Homeland Security more time to plan an arrest. The virus had forced the cell to alter their means of communication, which was later traced via an unsecured cell phone. The result were several arrests, as well as a nice *Washington Post* article about Michael and the clichéd writing regarding the overcoming of one's handicap and the ability to contribute to the betterment of our society. Michael was a modest guy and ignored the multitude of talk show requests.

Stephen got up, opened the front door, and said good-bye to

Michael's housemates. He wished them a fun weekend and told them to be careful out there, ever-quoting old TV and movie lines. He bent down over his brother and told him he loved him. His eyes dampened a bit as he turned and shuffled to his car. He wiped the tear from his eyes and headed home.

CHAPTER XXX

Rick woke from the short nap brought on by several shots of Jack on his empty stomach and gazed up at the clock. He decided to grab one of his disposable cell phones and try to reach Adrianna again. He tapped the numbers on the keypad and waited. On the third ring, a soft voice answered.

"Adrianna Falcone, whom may I ask has graced my phone line?"

The voice was void of any serious accent, or at least an obvious one. The inflection was steady, and there were no hints of anything recognizable. Bryant had mentioned she was originally from Philadelphia but had lived in different localities. The accent may have been nondescript, but the tone was sexy as hell.

"Good afternoon, Adrianna, it's Ri—"

"Do you prefer to be called Rick, Ricky, or Richard?" she interrupted, her voice displaying a teasing quality.

"Whatever you prefer, Adrianna," Rick almost timidly replied. He was mesmerized, and he had no clue why. "I usually go by Rick."

"I'm so sorry I wasn't able to answer your earlier call. I'm so glad you called back. I was actually looking forward to it. You have a nice voice."

"As do you," he replied, his voice gaining some of the strength that had earlier diminished from his tone. "Bryant told me about you, and after our ninety-second chat, I would like to meet you even more. Love the vibes!" Rick wished he could take back that overly anxious comment, but her reply shot back in seconds.

"What took you so long to ask?"

They both laughed, almost in perfect unison.

"A sense of humor too," he said. "I'll add that to the short list, which is growing larger by the second." He was acting like a kid, like he used to with Brandi. It felt natural, unrehearsed, and he loved it.

"Bryant mentioned that I'm both married and looking, I assume. Unfortunately, my husband and I have some plans, made well in advance, for this evening, but tomorrow couldn't be too soon. He's leaving for a business trip, which will grant me seven days of peace."

"What does your husband do, if I may ask?" He didn't really care all that much, but information was never a bad thing.

"He's in real estate, and quite a successful investment banker. He travels to evaluate different commercial properties that are either in foreclosure or unfinished. As you can guess, it keeps him busy. He travels nationally and to some Caribbean properties and is gone more time than he's here, which is one of the things I like best about him," she said with a hint of disdain in her voice. She continued. "I'm not boring you, Rick, am I?" she asked teasingly.

"No, please continue," he said, feigning interest.

"We'd moved into a small apartment in Narberth while waiting for our house to be completed, which it recently was. He thought that buying a five-bedroom English-style cottage might improve our crumbling marriage, but that is so far from reality. As far as I'm concerned, we are *so* done. After college, I worked for some high-end interior design firms, so the house was to be my special project, but to me, it's more like therapy. I need other interests, and it's certainly not his sorry ass, as he may believe." Her tone was pensive, and he liked the fact that she was confiding in him during their first conversation. Adrianna shifted the conversation. "Bryant mentioned you're single, and you seem so cool. Cool and single, how do you manage that? No lady get a ring strapped to you yet? Hold that topic for tomorrow night. Where shall we meet, Rick?"

Rick was still a bit enchanted. His mind quickly turned to where they could have a semiromantic rendezvous, not wanting to appear as interested as he was feeling. Almost without thinking he responded to her query. "I have a wonderful place in mind. Have you ever been to Georges', in Wayne?"

"Oh, that's a place I've wanted to try for the longest time. I'd love to, Rick." Her response came with an undulating enthusiasm.

"Georges' it will be," he responded in a more confident tone.

"Say seven or so for cocktails?" Her seductive voice was reeling him in.

"It's a date. How will I recognize you?"

"I think you'll know. Just my woman's intuition, but if it gets much past midnight, I'll call!" Again they both giggled, as if they were high school sweethearts. They exchanged farewells, Rick feeling his heart beating a little faster, his underwear stretching in a good way.

Rick didn't move for several seconds, starting to wonder about their brief exchange. The conversation had flowed. She sounded intelligent and realistic, with the right bit of humor added to the mix. Her inquisitiveness as to why he was not married was not uncommon for a good looking, successful guy in his midlife. He'd been asked that before. His answers varied in depth and detail depending on the situation. She had Brandi-like qualities—at least the qualities he assumed Brandi might have, thirty years later. As he had learned in the past, it was not worth projecting anything more than the upcoming initial get-together. Classifying and prejudging a person or situation only led to disappointment.

Rick got up and started to contemplate plans for the evening. He had pretty much sobered up and was starting to develop an appetite. He palmed the white top of a pill bottle and removed his usual Xanax. He pulled an Amstel Light from the fridge and swallowed the pill down with a mouthful.

He walked into the office and started up his desktop. He lit a cigarette and waited for his home page to appear. The wait was longer than usual as his antivirus screen alerted him to the fact it had prevented a threat from an unknown source. He shrugged it off and logged on to his sports betting account. He decided to head over to his go-to eatery, the Capital Grille. He could get his usual bar seat and watch the Phillies thrash the Pittsburgh Pirates. It was a 7:05 p.m. start and Cliff Lee was pitching, seeking his league-leading thirteenth win. Although playing away from home, he was a big favorite in the betting. It would cost $210 to win $100. A big spread, but Rick believed in a solid, locked-in play. He scrolled to the baseball page and clicked the box indicating the Phillies. He directed the mouse to the wager column and entered a sum of $1,000, which would win him slightly less than $500 when they won. He crushed out his cigarette, finished his beer, and changed into his jeans. He decided to drive the ten or so blocks, as a humid ninety degree haze engulfed the city and he didn't feel like walking.

Rick entered the bar area, nodding to the front staff and waving to some of the other regulars he sporadically exchanged pleasantries with. Rick was feeling kind of extravagant this evening, probably due to his perceived good vibes emanating from his earlier chat with Adrianna. After two shots of brandy, he ordered the lobster bisque, Iceberg wedge, and a porcini-rubbed rib eye.

The bisque arrived at the top of the third, neither team having advanced a runner past first base. The third Jack was starting to kick in when Pirates scored two unearned runs in the bottom of the fourth inning. Rick pushed his stool from the bar and headed outside for a good luck smoke. He crushed it out several minutes later and reclaimed his seat. The wedge arrived at the top of the fifth, with the score remaining 2–0. It was not that the loss would financially hurt Rick, but he hated the Phillies, or his bets, losing. He mopped up the last of the blue cheese dressing, his steak arriving with perfect timing. The Phillies cut the lead in half on a Chase Utley solo blast, and the Pirates remained one run ahead. Drink number five arrived as Rick shushed some noisy patrons.

His plate was cleared as the game entered the ninth. Rick grabbed a quick smoke outside as the Pirates made a pitching change. When he returned, the Phillies had a man on first with one out. With one strike on Utley, an outside fastball was hit hard down the first base line. Out of nowhere, the hard liner was caught as the first baseman stepped on the bag. In less than a second, the game was over with the double play.

Rick stood up, kicking the stool over, and sent a loud, "Fuck you!" toward the large plasma screen. Before he could be told to behave or leave, he threw $200 on the bar, leaving on his own accord.

His car arrived. He denied the offer of a cab, fell into the driver's seat, and was safely home in ten minutes. *I'd better behave tomorrow night*, he thought. *I can't live my life by the Phills. They can win and lose. I can only win.*

Two minutes later he was soundly asleep with his right sock dangling from his foot.

Chapter XXXI

Stephen Davis was woken a little after eight by his land line. He had not set his alarm as he was taking this Saturday off. This was his first day off in more than two weeks. He was planning on sleeping in, not even wanting to think.

He rolled over to the nightstand and glanced at the caller ID. The screen read *Michael*, and there was never a time he ignored a call from his younger brother. He was the only family Davis had, and he'd do anything for him. "Yo, bro," he said in an obviously half asleep sound.

"Stephen, you son of a Davis," came an obvious quote. The two siblings would usually quote movies at the start of a phone call. Today's ticket: *Fargo*.

"You're darned tootin'. Dontcha know," Stephen fired back.

"I have begun the project we had talked about and have found some malfeasance." He quoted Marge.

"Nice one, bro, you're on the top of your game. Give me a minute to take a leak and start Mr. Coffee. Be right back." Davis tossed the covers off and flew into the bathroom. He relieved himself and hustled into the kitchen to start the morning's octane brewing. "Talk to me, bro."

Michael obliged. "Very interesting guy this Rick Grosse is. He's also a very careful one. I broke down his searches into several categories. First, he's a major sports junkie, as well as a homer or home team fan. He checks all four of the home team's message boards and even posts sarcastic comments on occasion, rarely anything positive. He orders various things from Amazon, such as books, music, and memorabilia. He buys some hard-to-get tickets from various sites, but that's it."

The beeper on the coffee machine let Davis know the brewing was complete, and he told Michael to hold the next thought. Less than a minute later he was perched on the edge of the bed and asked Michael to go on.

"The next grouping was a little more interesting. He enjoys escort sites, spends a fair amount of time reading the ads, maybe doing some recruiting for some of his contacts. He dabbles in some sports betting, probably for business and pleasure. Again, nothing too racy or out of the ordinary here for any American adult male. Here's where we get a bit more interesting."

Davis sipped his coffee and slid closer to the edge of the bed, his interest starting to pique.

Michael knew he was being successful at building a crescendo of interest in his older brother. Firstly because Davis hadn't interrupted him more than thirty-five times, and secondly because he'd taken the time to make wake-up coffee in an effort to remain alert.

"I went through the case notes you loaned to me and found several questionable and relative searches. The first one was done several months ago. It queried commercial properties that were abandoned, for sale, or in the process of being demolished."

"Did the Philadelphia Zoo pop up in the search, or anything near Girard Avenue?" Davis asked.

"You betcha," Michael replied.

"Go on."

"Medical anesthetics, along with their properties and usage, also appeared. It contained a multitude of sedatives, narcotics, and hypnotics, followed by an ancillary search in the Physician's Desk Reference. He hasn't had any medical training, has he?"

"Not in this lifetime," came the response.

"These are just a synopsis. I've printed out a complete log of anything that fits the case of the homicide you guys are investigating. Should I fax it over?"

"Hang on to it, bro. Give me an hour; I'll pick you and the files up and take you both for breakfast. You're the best, and like I said, keep it between us girls, okay?"

Michael agreed and added he would be ready when his brother arrived. A day off for either was obviously not in the cards.

Davis got cleaned up and ready in what might have earned him a spot in the Guinness Book of Record, for the fastest time of morning readiness. His mind started to race, formulating to-do lists, team assignments, and possible warrants to explore. He decided to return to his office in order to put his ducks in a row. He would send a message to his team, requesting their presence at a Sunday working brunch. He needed time to organize, which is one of the tasks he did best. He did have to be careful, knowing his search was not really legal and information had been obtained in a fraudulent way. If the criminal did not play by the rules, why should he? This was one of his mantras, and so far, he'd played this game well. At least this gave him someplace to start. He'd worry about all the legalistic probing after he found out what he should be looking for.

Almost at the same time that Davis was driving downtown to the Roundhouse, Rick was waking up. His memories were a bit skewed in regard to the past evening, but he had been there before. He strode over to the desk and rolled up his office chair. He turned on the desktop and removed a key from the center draw. He inserted the key into the lock and slowly pulled the drawer several inches out. He removed a small white bag containing his breakfast. Along with his coffee, this would wake him up, giving him that extra needed lift. He returned the bag and straw to the drawer and pushed the button illuminating his desktop monitor. As had happened yesterday, his virus program was busy at work, cleaning up threats it had detected. Rick had seen this before. Unless the user was computer savvy, he would never suspect it had been breached.

On occasion he would do some people searches, especially when *Full Service Concierges* was dealing with new clients. He found one of the people search engines he had signed up for and typed in the name Adrianna Falcone.

The search light blinked with its low hum, eventually turning up two dozen or so matches. Ages and locations varied. Bryant had mentioned she had lived in several places, and he was clueless as to her exact age. He scrolled through the list of possibilities, but more than a dozen still remained. The coke and the coffee had kicked in, diminishing his patience to continue his detective work. Hell, he was a gambler, and she sounded okay. Actually better than okay. If this first encounter would lead anywhere, he would delve into her past in a more thorough nature.

He then did his daily inspection of the Philadelphia sports activities. He avoided last night's disaster with the Phillies, so he checked on the Eagles and 76ers to see if any off-season stories were newsworthy. He preferred reading an actual newspaper rather than the websites, but he liked reading during mealtime.

He decided to run some errands he'd been putting off. He needed some staples at the market, just in case he had late night company or needed to make a frittata for any guests he might seduce. He had some shirts at the dry cleaners, needed some cash for the evening, and his supply of Jack Daniels and brandy were almost depleted.

After several hours of navigating the empty city streets, he decided on a quick stop for his weekly cheese steak. He sat down at an outdoor wooded table, his trusty *Daily News* by his side. In the suburban section, he noticed that another robbery shooting had occurred less than a mile from where he'd committed his murder. He wondered, had he started a trend? Nah, Philly had been anchored in the top-ten list of large-city homicides for some time now. He tossed the pile of yellow-stained napkins into the large trash bin and cruised from South Philly back home.

Davis called Eckland, wanting to update him on the progress of the case. It was also his *supposed* day off. After eight run-on sentences, Eckland bellowed a loud "Yo!" through the phone's mouthpiece. "Davis, take a break, slow it down," he said. "Give it a rest for a night. Get in your car, and we can meet for a civilized dinner. We can mix in a little business, but let's just relax. We can sort it out tomorrow. Okay?" Eckland was pleading his case.

"Okay, you win and you're right. Where should we meet?"

They decided to meet at seven o'clock at Downey's, a multilevel pub located in Society Hill. In Davis's opinion this could not wait until Monday, much to Eckland's chagrin.

Now thoroughly awake, Eckland lay in bed wondering what his boss could possibly have been up to.

Chapter XXXII

Rick debated calling to confirm his meeting with Adrianna. If his instincts and gut feelings were in sync, a call would be unnecessary. Their date was at seven, and his adrenalin was starting to build. It had been a while since he'd been excited about meeting a new woman. His obsession with Brandi had served as a barometer, and no one had ever exceeded that level. It was an involuntary part of his being, much the same as breathing, and there was no cure. He was like Rick in *Casablanca*. His future plans and love for her had been aborted by fate, so he believed. Strands of guilt did play upon his emotions at times, regretting he hadn't followed his heart and found her, and, like a Hollywood ending, whisked her away and lived happily ever after. But everyone has regrets over missed opportunities in life.

He quickly dismissed those passing thoughts. Tonight was a new adventure, maybe even a new chapter that might banish Brandi from his thoughts forever. He opened his sliding walk-in closet door and removed the plastic wrap from his Alfani stone-corded silk blazer. It was his favorite. He matched it with slacks from the same designer and a Hugo Boss textured Clifford shirt in lavender. He passed by the full length mirror, admiring his stylish threads. He ran some gel and a brush through his messy locks and did a second pass by the mirror. He looked good and felt good. Just for good measure, he unlocked the desk draw for a quick snort, his evening ritual now complete.

About thirty miles north, Adrianna Falcone too was preparing for this special evening. She walked into her large ten foot by eighteen foot walk-in closet and sorted through the racks of designer outfits that occupied almost the whole front wall. She slid the garments from right to left, as if shopping in Nordstrom or Ann Taylor. She wanted a seductive, sleeveless dress that would turn heads, although that wasn't too difficult, even if she was wearing something off the rack at K-Mart. She stopped at a Ralph Lauren sleeveless sequined number with a crossover V-neckline. It was a light indigo, which highlighted her flowing hair. She slipped it on and gave herself a nod of approval. She decided to add a Nine West floppy wine-colored hat, giving her an air of mystique and drama. For the final touch, she chose a pair of Nina Cerelia evening sandals, complete with a constellation of rhinestone details. The shoes were sinfully seductive. Any American male would refer to them as CFM, or come-fuck-me, shoes. As did Rick, she gave her appearance a second nod of approval.

She returned to her spacious bedroom and gathered the assorted items that occupy any woman's handbag essentials. She filled it with makeup, a small compact, lipstick, cigarettes, cell phone, and the six hundred other oddities needed for an evening out. She grabbed the car keys off the nightstand and strode to the three-car garage. She opened the door of her Lexus, standard transportation for a Mainline resident, and pushed the automatic garage door opener. She slowly backed out onto the street, setting her course for a long awaited rendezvous.

She knew about Georges', located in Wayne, Pennsylvania. The world-renowned chef and owner, George Perrier, has combined eclectic gourmet food with an environment complete with twelve foot ceilings, a sun lit indoor courtyard and an outdoor patio.

Adrianna arrived ten minutes early, surrendering her car to a gawking valet, and rewarded him with a seductive smile. Blushing, he took the keys and drove the car toward the parking area.

Upon entering, she mentioned to the hostess that if a solo gentleman walked in looking for a woman to please tell him she was in the bar. She then turned left into the spacious room, admiring the country feel that was formed by the vaulted ceilings. She glanced at the long bar and found two unoccupied seats at the end. The French doors on the left gave a glimpse of the entering patrons.

A well manicured bartender slid a napkin toward her, asking in a pleasant voice, "A cocktail for the lady? Perhaps some wine?"

"That would be lovely, Eric," she replied, glancing at his gold embossed name plate. She glanced at the signature Martini placard and contemplated her choice. "May I please have a chocolate martini, Grey Goose if you will?"

"Certainly, madam," Eric replied in a slightly subservient tone, appreciated by many of the condescending, arrogant patrons. Eric momentarily returned with the standard shaped martini glass and placed it on the napkin in front of Adrianna. She raised the glass to her lips as Eric watched. A wide smile of satisfaction appeared on her lips.

"Don't quit your night job, Eric; this drink is divine."

"Thank you. It's rare I get a compliment in here. I'm glad you're enjoying it. Would you care to see a menu?"

"No thank you. I'm waiting for a friend to arrive. Thank you anyway; you're so sweet."

Eric headed over to a party of two who approached the two empty stools at the other end of the bar. At that same moment, Adrianna turned her gaze to the window and saw a well dressed middle-aged man approach the entrance. At that moment, she noticed that her past emotions and thoughts eerily erupted throughout her whole being. As quickly as they appeared, she shut them out. She closed her eyes. *Game time*, she said quietly to herself, as she turned back toward the bar and sat up in her stool.

Rick entered the restaurant and checked in with the hostess. On cue, she inquired if he was meeting a woman here. He nodded, and she mentioned she was waiting at the bar. He approached the only remaining empty stool next to a woman who may be Adrianna. His left hand gripped the back of the empty stool. His right hand slid onto the back of the woman's chair to the right. She leaned back against the arm Rick had draped behind her. Rick felt her soft skin that remained uncovered by her dress, touch the back of his hand. At that instant, Rick felt like he'd been struck by an unearthly power. As they turned to look at each other, Rick's heart felt like it would propel through his chest and into eternity. Neither of them emitted a sound, their eyes seemingly attached in a vice-like embrace.

Rick, who was rarely speechless, uttered the first sound. "It can't be, can't be. Brandi?" his voice trembling, barely above a whisper.

"Ricky, my God. This is unreal." She stuttered, mostly because her emotions startled her. She strove to mirror his surprise. She had to make him believe how shocked she acted.

"This is like a fairy tale. For more than thirty years you have never, ever left my thoughts, my being. Never. You are an answer to my prayers." He paused. "You are more beautiful than ever, a goddess." His voice oozed sincerity, lust, and surprise.

"Ricky. This is beyond anything I could have imagined." Her reply and inflections conveyed a genuine feel.

"Brandi. I had this feeling, this, I don't know what it was, after we spoke. I would have never guessed in a million years."

She pulled the martini glass up to her lips, swallowing the remaining contents in one smooth motion.

"Why Adrianna? Where have you been? What—"

She put her index finger over his lips, stopping his speech as quickly as a bullet.

"Let's get our table and talk. I know you have a lot of questions, as do I. We have all evening, unless you can't stand the sight of me." Her remark was obviously meant to be a tease.

Rick stared intensely at her, like a child seeing his missing pet come home after all hope had been lost. He asked her what she was drinking as he pulled a large (attempt to impress) roll of cash from his front pocket.

"Double chocolate Grey Goose martini," she replied, calling Eric over. He caught her request and approached the couple, politely asking Rick if would care for a drink.

"Double shot of bran—" He paused, looked at her, and changed his mind. "Triple Jack, straight up," he replied. The shock of Brandi, or Adrianna, or whatever she called herself, was waning and it was time for a reality check.

When Eric returned, Rick asked for the check. Glancing over at it, he peeled off a fifty dollar bill and placed it on the bar. As Eric reached for it, he told him to keep the change because he couldn't think of waiting to get a table.

They proceeded to the hostess stand. Rick mentioned his name and the hostess grabbed two menus, asking the pair to follow her. They were placed at a table overlooking the patio, a good view for watching the panoramic motions of the night sky. But then who was thinking about the view? Even as Brandi pretended to look about, he was trapped in his thoughts.

For the next several seconds, which seemed like an eternity, Rick sat with a childlike gaze fixed on Brandi. Regaining his composure and thoughts, he said, "So many years have gone by, Brandi. We have hundreds stories, thoughts, and experiences to share. At least I do. Where can we begin?" His tone was both inquisitive and sincere.

She raised her glass for a toast, trying to regain her composure, as well as slowing things down.

"To the past, the present, and ..." her voice trailed off for effect.

The familiar sound of glasses clinking signified the sort of union, or at least reunion, they were in the midst of sharing. They simultaneously lifted their cocktails. With broad smiles, they sipped together, as they had done long, long ago.

The waiter unintentionally interrupted the mood, unaware of the monumental event that had just taken place.

"Would either of you care for another cocktail?" William, the server asked in a droning voice. Brandi chimed in first, opting for a chilled double shot of Grey Goose, not being in the mood for the chocolate or the calories. Rick reduced his order to a double shot of Knob Creek, not minding to mix his bourbons. The waiter handed them menus, promising to return shortly with the daily specials. Rick suggested they peruse the menus so they could order when William returned, reducing the time they might be interrupted.

They alternated glances at the menu and each other. Regardless of what Brandi felt would happen, past memories and the good feelings of youth slowly crept into the equation.

Rick was lost in the moment. For so many years he'd yearned to see her again, and now his dreams had transformed into reality.

"They don't write scripts like this in Tinsel Town these days," he said to Brandi in a serious tone. "Who woulda thunk?"

"Was that a Yogi Berra or Casey Stengel quote?" she asked, remembering his youthful affinity for baseball.

"Hell if I can remember, but it fits the moment."

William returned, carrying the two cocktails. Brandi observed the two contrasting colors of the liquids. She thought about Rick and his bourbon, its dark amber tint and the crystal clear of her own vodka. How different they were.

William placed the drinks easily accessible to the patrons. He recited the short list of daily specials by memory, asked if they had any questions about the menu, and stood at the ready for their orders.

Brandi suggested Rick choose a first course for them, mentioning she would enjoy any of his selections. She knew that her sincerity and submissive behavior would eventually disarm her first lover.

With his masculinity successfully and unknowingly stroked, he sat up in his chair before speaking, his body language striving to show both confidence and even a hint of dominance.

Damn I'm good, Brandi thought.

"As long as they're fresh, we'd like the chef's selected oysters. What is that expression? Eat oysters, live longer? Or is it love longer?"

Brandi let out a small laugh along with Rick. She sensed that the comfort level was rising, as well as her subtle manipulations. Rick quashed his urge for the cheese steak spring rolls.

Turning to Brandi, William waited for her choice.

"I would like the heirloom tomato and mozzarella salad to start. For my entrée, the roasted Branzino sounds divine."

William chimed in. "It's one of our most popular selections. Good choice, ma'am. And for you, sir?"

"Thanks, William. I'd like the onion soup to begin and the braised beef short ribs to follow. But would you mind substituting some French fries for the vegetables, please?" Rick ignored the no-substitutions-in an-overpriced-French-restaurant rule.

"Glad to, sir," William replied in the all too subservient Mainline response. William asked if there would be anything else, and when no answer was given, he left the two alone.

Rick said, "Over the past thirty or so years, rarely a day goes by without regrets, my regrets for screwing things up. I know it's late and we can't go back in time, but I'm *so* sorry for my lack of responsibility.

It's something that will haunt me for eternity." He reached across the table; he wanted to take her hand in his. Brandi pulled away.

"And you very well should!" Brandi said with a piercing growl. "I know. We were young, stupid, and all those other overused clichés, but damn it, Rick, you didn't step up. You tore my heart to pieces!" Her head turned to the window; she dabbed her eyes with a quick finger.

Rick was hoping this subject would stay dormant for at least until the main course, but Brandi had come out swinging.

She continued. "I was whisked out of town, away from my friends, family, and school, all the stability a young kid needs to have. And at no time, not once, did you express any remorse or take any responsibility for what happened. You ignored me and the situation, which makes it *so* hard to forgive you. You hurt me with a pain that never goes away." Her voice was trembling a bit, delivering an emotional spear that pierced his manliness to its core.

In an emotional and remorseful voice, Rick countered. "I know that sorry won't cut it or make you forgive me or my actions. I was irresponsible, immature, and stupid. I fucked up. The hurt I caused you I also inflicted upon myself. The funny thing is, I've never forgiven myself and have carried it with me like a cross. If this is our last contact, I'll totally understand. All I can offer is my deepest regrets and sincerest apologies."

"I didn't know what your reaction would be when I threw this all at you, but at least you've become a man and realize the pain you've caused. This has been bothering me too for all this time. I've learned a lot from this. It's made me more cautious, less trusting, and a hell of a lot more independent. I almost stood you up tonight, but I suppose what we had in the past still must mean something to me."

Rick had no idea what to expect for an answer as he prepared to ask what might be a touchy question. He proceeded slowly, and with extreme caution. "Might I ask what happened with … well, your pregnancy?"

Brandi knew that question was not far from following her diatribe and was poised for his question.

"I lost the baby during childbirth. I cut out the drinking and drugs after leaving Philadelphia. The doctor said there might have been a problem because of the sudden cold-turkey quit. At first I didn't care what happened. I almost ran away to have an abortion, but my family said they would do anything for me if I didn't abort. It was traumatic, and I *wanted* to talk to you—the father—about it but just couldn't. It also didn't help that my parents hated you and felt you had deserted me."

Rick's emotions started to show up in the form of tears running from his now reddened eyes. Brandi too was getting emotional. All of the rage and the hate were now being released like an erupting volcano. Rick reached for Brandi's hand on the table again. He stroked it softly and then embraced it with a heartfelt squeeze. He had never imagined their reunion would evoke these terrible memories, which he had ignored since she'd moved away.

Brandi took a deep breath, sighed, and let out her breath as if it was releasing all the hurt that had built up inside her. She squeezed back, conveying a small sign of accepting his mistakes and regrets.

"Can we go have a cigarette, Rick? I really need one after that."

Rick almost jumped out of his seat, circling around the table in order to pull her chair away as she arose. "At your service, m'lady," he said in a poor attempt at a British accent.

"Thank you, my lord," her response being much more authentic, as well as breaking the mounting tensions.

They exited the restaurant toward the patio, Rick's arm placed gently on her back, offering a hint of compassion.

Brandi reached into her cramped purse as Rick pulled his pack of smokes from his inside jacket pocket. Rick removed his lighter and they both leaned in, touching the flickering flame, and tugging in the first taste of smoke. Their eyes met, and suddenly to Rick it was like old times were resurrected and living well in Philadelphia. As they smoked, they took turns recounting the past as well as filling in the blanks on the missing years.

They casually strolled back to their table to await the main course. Rick thought that it was a rekindling of the past, a new start. Brandi's thoughts and feelings were quite the opposite.

William observantly saw the pair return and headed to the kitchen to retrieve their main course. He arrived with an exquisitely plated presentation. They both smiled in approval and commented on how good dinner looked. The conversation continued without any more emotional outbursts.

Brandi gave Rick an abbreviated version of her time post Philadelphia to the present. She started in Indiana and went to college at Indiana University. She graduated with a degree in English, screwed a lot of guys, waitressed, and then took some courses in interior design. She took a liking to it and worked in Boston and then in Baltimore. She said she'd made her worst mistake ever when she foolishly fell for a hotshot real estate guy she'd met at a bar in Baltimore. After a few years of marriage she realized it had been a big mistake. "At the present, I'm enjoying dinner with an old friend and don't know what the future holds."

She knew Rick would interpret this statement as a "go" sign. That was just fine with her. In fact it was more than fine, it was perfect.

When it was Rick's turn to narrate his biography, it was void of many of the unsavory details. He told her about his post-high school loathing, his short time locked up, and bits and pieces about his business with Carl. He embellished the story with a fictional account about his theory of Carl's demise. He left out such trivial stories such as St. Maarten, Bryant Merril, and Gando. Maybe later he'd share those.

They decided to return to the bar for one more drink as it was only slightly past ten. Eric welcomed Brandi back, and she introduced Rick as they slid into two empty bar stools. The two exchanged pleasantries. Eric asked what they would like and waited for the response.

"Bring us a bottle of Dom Perignon Eric, if that's okay with the lady," he requested.

"No need to ask," Brandi interrupted, acknowledging Rick's perfect choice. A minute later he returned with a highly polished bucket and two glasses. Eric unleashed the cork, a slight misty wisp emerging from the opening. He poured, ladies first of course, and then wrapped the bottle in a fresh napkin before returning it to the iced container.

He raised his glass, and staring into her eyes, whispered, "To the most wonderful woman who has ever graced this planet."

Brandi gave the impression of modesty and appreciation for the overly generous salutation. "You are way too kind, but as romantic as ever, my old friend," And with that, their glasses ceremoniously met before they sipped the bubbly.

"I do have one question," Rick mused. "Why Adrianna?"

Brandi tried to hide an emerging smile of guilt before her reply. "Just as you've skipped many details of your past, let's save the long version for another time. The abbreviated version is that I needed to get away from a particular situation, and a name and location change seemed the best way."

Rick accepted the evasive answer. After all, she was right. He too was giving her abridged versions of his past.

"Touché!" he countered, and they both continued the quest of emptying the bottle.

They conversed almost nonstop, with laughter, seriousness, and interest filling their conversation. When the bottle was done, Rick slid his arm on the backrest of the stool. He leaned closer and asked in a low voice, "I really hope we can keep the evening going."

Without hesitation, Brandi replied, "Okay, buster, let's get out of this place. And in the meantime, cross your legs. You're becoming indecent enough that the other ladies are jealous."

Rick was encouraged by her immediate and observant reply. He thought it better to leave her comment alone while he was way ahead of his earlier expectations. He summoned Eric and requested the check. Brandi insisted on picking this one up, mentioning that it was all her husband's money anyway. She peeled off two Ben Franklins, and taking a card from her purse, handed it to Rick.

"In case we get separated driving, here's the address. Meet you there when I meet you there!"

He leaned over to give her a small kiss on the cheek and rose from the bar.

"This night is beyond description. It's just so—"

Brandi put her finger to his lips, acknowledging his sincerity and excitement. They left the bar and waited for the valets to retrieve their vehicles.

Chapter XXXIII

The two-lane ride down Route 1 was laden with red lights and moderate Saturday night traffic. Rick followed Brandi through each traffic light, none of them impeding his progress as if by some divine intervention. He slipped his 80s CD into the player, his fingers keeping a steady beat as Rod Stewart's version of "Young Turks" transposed him back to past memories. He was still dumbfounded in regard to what had transpired over the past several hours. *How the hell did this happen?* he thought. It was a Hollywood script, whereas life couldn't have imitated art any better. No matter. He was following his lifelong love and obsession. He was sure that fate had orchestrated the whole scenario, and if not, who cared?

Fifteen minutes and several towns later, he began followed her through a maze of spacious homes and properties where the "other half" lived. Towering homes with three-car garages, copper-domed roofs, and three-story Doric columns decorated expensive gaudy homes. Lawns were precisely manicured, as if each blade of grass was individually measured.

They turned to a ten-foot wrought iron gate. Her brake lights intensified as her car slowed to a rolling stop. She turned at the next driveway, harboring a classy country styled residence. He pulled up behind her and shut down the engine. She emerged slowly, giving Rick time to catch up before entering.

"Welcome to my world," Brandi said in a slightly sarcastic tone.

"What, no gargoyles or tacky fountains? I thought you were a decorator!"

Brandi laughed softly, giving Rick a harmless elbow to the ribs.

"I haven't lived here long enough to outdo my neighbor's poor taste. Give me a couple of months to best my neighbors in decreasing my property value."

She withdrew the keys from her bag and opened the large oak doors. Grabbing his hand, she guided him into the darkened foyer and reached for the light switch. She turned the dimmer, shedding light on the spacious entryway. The space was mostly barren of decorations, due to the fact that the home was still a project in the making. The next burst of light produced a large living room complete with a sixty inch plasma screen, top-of-the-line home theater equipment, and several curved suede couches. The décor was modern, the glossy hardwood floor making the room appear even larger. Several abstract prints adorned the textured walls.

Rick tugged on her hand, drawing her closer. His placed his right hand behind her head and drew her face into his. Without hesitation, their lips met as if some magnetic force pulled them together. Feeling the warm softness of her lips, their tongues began dancing together in a playful rhythm. Lust, passion, and memories filled his senses as pure pleasure engulfed him. Brandi slowly withdrew, her breathing more pronounced. She rolled her eyes and smiled.

"We haven't lost a step, have we, Ricky?" she bantered.

"Hell no," he quickly replied, now feeling lightheaded. His desires heightened. No need to mention he went by the more masculine "Rick" now.

She offered to give him a quick tour, slowing down the pace of what they both knew was to follow. "Would you care for a drink?" she asked, their eyes only focused on each other.

"Love one," he replied in a hypnotic tone.

They approached the built-in bar area, tucked away in the far corner of the living room area. She lifted the bottle of bourbon without asking and began to pour a generous amount. Rick stopped her halfway.

"Actually, I go for brandy now," he said with a grin.

She smiled even wider and switched out the glass with a new one. She lifted the tongs and the lid off the bucket, but Rick's eyes conveyed he preferred it neat. She replaced the bottle and poured herself an equal amount of Grey Goose, her obvious vodka of choice. She dropped in two clouded cubes of ice, lifting her glass in the direction of his.

"To the unexpected and the uncontrolled," she gleefully exclaimed.

"Stated with such charm and grace, just as I have always remembered," his compliment appearing to her as a bit of a line, yet with his obvious admiration.

With drinks in hand, she offered to continue the tour of the second floor. *Talk about obvious*, she thought. Like a new puppy not yet housebroken, Rick silently followed her up the broad spiral staircase upstairs.

It was like old times. Rick knew it was his stairway to heaven.

Abbreviating the proposed tour, she opened the door to a large bedroom. Black and white lacquered furniture blended with bright multicolored area rugs, all tied together with soft, multidirectional track lights. A large window overlooked the pool, sun room, and well tended shrubbery. Tall Alaskan firs gave an eerie yet seductive feel to the picturesque setting.

As they stood face to face, she slowly approached him. Placing her hands gently on his waist, she nudged him backward toward the large king-sized bed. He offered no resistance, mesmerized by the power she held over him. When he could go no further, he fell onto the edge of the bed, being lifted once by the firm springs. With a deliberate forward motion she pushed him onto his back, with no resistance being offered. Her lips covered his mouth, initiating the start of a passion-filled encounter. She positioned her body on top of his, sliding back and forth in a synchronized and seductive motion. His breathing increased, emitting soft, uncontrollable sounds of pleasure.

They tore their clothes off as if they had been set on fire. Her nails dug into his chest, leaving red lines behind, like chalk on a freshly cleaned blackboard. During the next several hours they took turns pleasing each other in an unselfish manner. They satisfied each other several times, combining their physical movements with short bursts of erotically provocative dialogue. The moment yielded laughter, intensity, and passion, as well as carnal satisfaction. When they were finally too tired to continue, the collapsed side by side, drifting into a satisfied respite. It was a night Rick would never forget.

The following morning Rick woke to the aroma of freshly brewing coffee, accompanied by the distinct smell of sizzling bacon. He sat up to find an apparently new terrycloth bathrobe neatly folded at the edge of the bed. He planted his feet on the floor, his euphoric feelings still fresh in his mind and body. He put on the robe and followed his sense of smell to its origin, down the circular stairs.

He easily found the large, sunlit kitchen. A rose tinted slab of granite served as the top of the table which stood centered in the large kitchen. It was obvious that Brandi had developed culinary interests over the past thirty years, though he doubted her spouse ever had time for a home-cooked meal.

"Good morning, my friend," Brandi greeted him cheerfully.

"Is it really morning? I want a do-over from last night. As a matter of fact, we can do it over forever as far as I'm concerned."

"Oh can we? You may not want to *every* night," she continued.

"Oh yes I could, and would," he replied, an overabundance of emotion stressed in his statement.

"Let's have some breakfast by the pool and then we can figure out what's next."

He agreed and waited to help her carry a tray outside.

Chapter XXXIV

That same morning, the OCTF gathered in conference room C in the Roundhouse's all too familiar surroundings. Davis was excited about some new breaking developments he would share with the team. But he knew he couldn't share the source, his brother. He promised a brief meeting, maybe only lasting an hour or so, but when the flipchart stood at the front of the room, they knew it might turn into a marathon.

A rising chatter filled the room. The standard Dunkin' Donuts boxes were absent, replaced by boxes decorated with the Panera Bread logo.

"Yo, Davis! Since when did you go gourmet and try to break us from our beloved Dunkin' addiction?" The comment was tossed in by Gina Vegas, and on-again off-again team member who was just returning from an undercover assignment. She'd been bartending at a known hangout down in South Philly, assigned to investigate a splinter group of tough guys working for a New York family trying to expand into the city.

Davis thanked the group for giving up some of their free time, which explained the boxes full of bear claws, brownies, pecan rolls, and bacon and egg soufflés. Both the wisecracks and clamor subsided as Davis approached the blank flipchart, purple marker at the ready.

"Thank you all for coming down today, and I mean that sincerely."

Several *your welcomes, is this overtime?,* and *you owe us big time* resounded from the group.

He approached the easel. "Some new developments have risen in regard to the Mickels case. You all know how personally I'm taking this, and we also know that scumbag Grosse is responsible."

Nodding heads and expressions of agreement sprang from the group.

"We will be taking some new approaches to the case. First, we need to go over all of Grosse's medical connections and contacts. That sedative is a highly controlled substance, and it can't be that difficult to track. By the way, after I present our new approach, Geek will team you up for the investigation.

"Second, we need to take a closer look at all bank accounts and associated transactions. Grosse has been out of commission for a while, is used to living large, and has no ongoing source of bringing home the bacon. Let's delve a little deeper. I also want you to step up the pressure on our informants. The street speaks volumes, and we're not hearing what it's saying. Start digging deeper, make some threats or make some deals, but learn whatever you can.

"I also want to start some tails and surveillance. We'll be watching Ms. Abbey Road. She's his alibi, business associate, and apparent lover. My gut says she's hiding something. Last month we placed a device on Grosse's car. Ellen Sue and I will start following him on Monday.

"We'll also try for a warrant to get his computer, cell accounts, and credit card receipts."

Over the next half hour several other impending and emerging cases were discussed. There were no major high-profile media cases at this moment, which was a rare occurrence during summertime in the City of Brotherly Love.

The meeting wound down with no significant discussions, and Davis told them to have a nice day off. It had been an atypical, less than two hour meeting, and Monday would initiate the renewed intensity to solve an open case.

Chapter XXXV

As Rick and Brandi relaxed in the Eden-like backyard décor, they continued catching up on the past two-plus decades.

"Why the name Adrianna Falcone?" Rick asked in an inquisitive manner. "Its obvious you've skimmed some things, Brandi, why not just tell me?"

Fully expecting this question, she prefaced a non abbreviated version. "In order for you to best understand, let me fill you on the years after my parents' whisked me away from you and Philadelphia."

Rick withdrew a cigarette from his pack and offered her one along with a light, indicating he was ready to listen.

"It was very hard at first, being away from school, you and all the familiarities that I had gotten accustomed to. Still being young and impressionable, I had two directions I could have chosen. I could have conformed, fit in, and been a goody two-shoes. You know damn well that was not who I was. Or I could have been a bit more irresponsible and rebellious, the other extreme, which wasn't really me either. Back here, I was a little of both."

Rick drew deeply on his cigarette, the smoke exiting his mouth as he started to ask a question. "How hard was it to adjust to such a nowhere kind of place?"

She smiled, indicating his spot on assessment of her being at that particular time of her life. Withdrawing the escaping ball of smoke, she looked upward, blowing a stream straight above Rick's head. "I chose the latter path, hoping that my sudden tantrums, outbursts, and disregard for my parents' new rules would make them give up and drag me back east. On the contrary. They informed me that as long as I behaved in such a manner, I would never get out of Dodge. During senior year I changed my tune, planning to leave as soon as I had my child and turned eighteen. I was young and stupid, as well as determined and naïve."

Rick hardly moved a muscle or offered any inkling of a response. His above-average memory was processing and storing all the information he was hearing.

Her eyes began to redden as the story continued. "I had never mentioned this to you, but my mother had miscarried twice before she had me. That same fate was passed onto me," her tone now fluctuated, her words intermittently crackling.

Rick sat speechless, the power of her hurt casing him pain. He began to speak but was abruptly cut off.

"I was a mess. I didn't know whether to find you and tell you, or find you and kill you. I obviously chose the former." Her voice had noticeably regained composure. "The next years at college I tried to straighten myself out. For two years I did. The third year I met a guy I fell for. One of those bad boys, and by the way, my instincts tells me you have a bit of that in you too!"

"No comments till later, and please go on, Brandi."

"I started partying a bit too much and got a little too involved in his affairs. On the surface, I thought it was just some midrange dealing, but he was hooked up with guns, importing, and worse. He began to lose it, becoming ultra paranoid, not even trusting me. One day while he was away on some big-time deal, I packed my shit and took off east. I grabbed a bit of cash from our joint account. Two days later I arrived in Boston. It was a young college town and I thought I could blend in better, take some night classes to finish school, eventually get my act together. That's when I legally changed my name, changed my hair color, and had my breasts enlarged. Hell, I'd run off with $25,000."

Rick sat back, processing the story he had just heard. It sounded like it could be the truth or a fabrication. He put it on his mental to-do list.

"I finished school, had several decorating jobs, met my husband, and here I sit," she said, studying his face in order to gauge her storytelling ability. "And if I was Santa, and you were sitting in my lap, would you tell me if you've been bad or good? It's your turn, Rick, and I'm curious to know how and why you met my friend Bryant Merril."

He knew he had to fill in the blanks from the abbreviated version of the missing years that he'd omitted the previous evening. But there was also only so much he could share because of Bryant and Gando.

"I would love a drink please, Brandi," Rick requested, partially to make the truth easier to convey, and partially because he loved a morning cocktail.

Brandi walked toward the bar area and poured them both a stiff wake-up shot. She handed him a drink, toasting his glass, and then took her place on the chair beside him.

Rick sat back and began to tell of his post-high school adventures, how he had enjoyed hustling, scamming, and being a creative entrepreneur. He told of his brief incarcerations as a guest of the state, downplaying the seriousness of his offenses. His recounting of the past amused Brandi, combining his successes and failures in an entertaining way. Her attention remained focused, soaking up his accounts as quickly as he detailed them. Just as he began talking about his partnership with Carl, she interrupted, offering to refill his empty glass.

"I had been following the case about Carl. Knowing how you two were good friends way back when, I wondered if you might have been involved, or for that matter, in danger?" Her tone was both sincere and accusatory.

"Involved? Not a chance. In danger, I sure as hell hope not. No one has contacted or threatened me, except the cops." His reply and tone attempted to denote innocence.

"Go on," she replied with interest.

"We had a business, *Full Service Concierges*. It was a service to some regulars, referrals and visitors to the city. We supplied bookies, hard-to-get venues, escorts, drugs, and the like. Our connections were many, but we strayed from anything too violent or over-the-top. We didn't strictly deal with goodie two-shoes but were careful to not bring attention to ourselves."

Lighting another cigarette, he continued. "Word on the street said that Carl had crossed the line with the wrong people, and because of that our partnership was instantly dissolved."

Brandi reclined in the chaise, sipped her drink, and asked, "Was Bryant Merril one of your clients or one of his?"

Rick pondered his next response. He wanted so much to be honest with her, but at the same time didn't want to scare her away by confessing his recent spree of evil. In no way did he want to even mention Julian, fearing that any leak of this critical information would be his last.

His belated response elicited a second comment from Brandi. "You do know that her husband was killed in a robbery gone bad several weeks ago?" Her tone had something behind it that had him concerned.

Rick sighed. "Yes I do know, but that's not really a concern of mine. I never even knew the guy." Avoidance glared through his response.

"Just curious," she stated calmly. "Funny thing is, I wish it could have been my good-for-nothing spouse instead."

This comment sent Rick's thoughts into a macabre reality. His reply was as subtle as an atomic bomb. "And if it were?"

"Then who's to say if we would be sharing breakfast for weekends to come?" Her response could be likened to an angler throwing out a line into a lake stocked with fish who hadn't eaten for months. They remained silent, waiting for each other to lead the conversation into a dark area, which they both had now entered.

"Suppose, and of course, this is all hypothetical, your husband, what's his name?"

"Leyland, but everyone calls him Lee," her response came, waiting for his to continue.

Rick's emotions were beginning to interfere with his usual logic. He was no match for a master manipulator, especially one of the feminine varieties.

For the next several moments, they both sat silent again. Without any prompting, Brandi got up and returned carrying the half empty bottle of brandy, the first half working as well as had expected. Rick smiled as she replenished his morning shot and joined him for another cigarette. She noticed that these two vices, when plied in unison, heightened both his cunning and courage. *No need for the waterboarding torture,* she joked to herself. *He's so damn easy.*

"Suppose what, Rick?" she said, prompting him to continue his train of thought.

His thoughts in order, Rick continued. "Your husband, Lee, meets an unfortunate and untimely death. A horrific and tragic accident. You become the bereaved widow. All alone. Devastated by his untimely loss. By some strange, fateful occurrence an old friend and lover suddenly reenters your life. And then?"

"Why, they live happily ever after, of course!" Her answer penetrated his soul with pinpoint accuracy.

Rick exhaled, full of thought and relief. He rose from his chair and began to pace. "If I may be so bold, may I assume the next step would be to formulate a *hypothetical* plan?"

"Yes, you may, Ricky, dear." Her response succeeded as a confirmation as well as a go ahead.

They both stirred, Brandi suggesting they move into the living room as the midmorning humidity was beginning to get uncomfortable. Rick mentioned he needed to run out to the car to grab some more smokes. Brandi nodded, saying she wanted to do a quick change. They both departed on their separate missions and would momentarily pick up where they had left off.

As Brandi navigated the stairs, she gave herself imaginary high fives, accomplishing her ultimate mission. She had put the wheels in motion, knowing Rick was now eager to step into her husband's place.

As he cut through the garage, Rick was confident about his ability to get away with murder and reap the benefits of his actions. They were on the same page, but each with a different motive.

Chapter XXXVI

Fewer than five minutes later, they both returned. Brandi sported a fresher, sexier look, and Rick had his chemical inspirations for planning a murder. Brandi sat across the glass table from Rick, watching as he extracted a small plastic bag filled with a white powder.

"Care to join me? It tends to speed up my creative thought process," Rick idyllically stated, as he poured some of the drugs.

"Thanks, but no thanks," she replied. "One of us should have a clear frame of mind."

"Cards on the table," Rick stated emphatically. "Truth is I have never stopped thinking about you. My thoughts consumed with fantasies, which you bestowed upon me last evening. I will do anything it takes to make the past up to you, as well as to never have you leave me again." Rick's tone was as serious and sincere as one could be. "Committing murder is a risk I will take, as long as it means never losing you to anyone. At anytime."

Brandi displayed an appreciative smile, saying she was flattered. "Rick, dear, have you ever seen this movie called *Double Indemnity?*"

"No, why?" he replied.

"It reminds me of what we're planning," she began. "The movie took place in the forties or fifties. In the original, Fred MacMurray, an insurance salesman, and Barbara Stanwyck, have a chance encounter when he visits her to renew her husband's life insurance. In a nutshell, they fall in love, plan to kill her husband, and then live happily ever after. The problem is, they leave too many loose ends, she shoots him, and they both wind up with nothing. In other words, we have to rewrite the script, avoiding any mistakes that cause us to come up with nada."

Rick mentioned that he might have seen bits and pieces of it but that he was the cautious type and was not known for making stupid mistakes. He stopped his overconfidence in its tracks, not wanting to reveal his 2–0 record in the homicide league. He asked for Brandi to gather him a notepad and pen so they could jot some ideas down to expound upon later. She retrieved his pad, pen, clean ashtray, and the remaining bottles of unfinished liquor.

Through the better part of the morning and into the afternoon, they tossed around various methods of murder that they believed would be less incriminating and obvious. The list on the pad slowly grew:

Drive-by shooting
Home accident
Hit and run
Car accident, brake line, flat tire, etc.
Poisoning
Home invasion or robbery
Paid hit man or assassin
Drug overdose
DUI
Bombing

As the day progressed, each scenario was discussed. They tried to poke holes in each of the actions, as to how they could slip up as well as how they could succeed. The levels in each bottle decreased by the hour, and the powder in the bag lessened as well. As the blue sky changed into its sunset hues, the lists were narrowed down to two alternatives: paid hit or home robbery. Brandi and Rick were skeptical about adding a third party to the mix, and they eventually declared home robbery the winner. They rose from the table and strolled into the backyard, hand-in-hand, a new confidence embedded in their walk.

"I haven't pulled an all-nighter since college, but I'm sure as hell ready."

They laughed, embraced, and kissed. It was their way of sealing the deal. After all, it was a lot sexier than a handshake.

Realizing they had not eaten since breakfast and were in no mood or condition to drive anywhere, they rummaged through the modestly stocked refrigerator. They picked at last night's leftovers, a partially wilted salad, and some Mediterranean chicken remaining from the Whole Foods takeout bar. With their minds exhausted and bodies not far behind, they climbed the stairs toward the bedroom. An encore performance from the previous evening would have them asleep in no time. Mission accomplished.

The next morning they woke, eager to tweak the script for Lee's final appearance in life. Unbeknownst to Rick, Brandi had woken an hour earlier. She had slipped over to the local deli, grabbing several assorted bagels and cream cheese. The aroma produced by the Tassimo brewing system permeated the house with a distinctly hazelnut bouquet. Rick grinned.

Brandi noticed, giving him a playful nudge and asking, "Okay, mister, why the shit-eating grin?"

"Just thinking about how awesome the past two days have been. And how awesome the next two and the next two …"

She smiled, telling him that she wholeheartedly agreed. "And when we have successfully completed our plan, those days will never end."

He turned and planted his lips on hers, gently sucking as his tongue ran below her upper one. She took a deep breath, breaking the hypnotic state that was beginning to take hold of her, and slowly pulled away.

"Put on some clothes and let's go eat. I'm famished," she huffed, tossing the fluffy comforter away from her body.

Rick followed and put on the robe draped over the ottoman.

Arriving in the kitchen, Rick found the cabinet containing the coffee mugs while Brandi sliced several bagels.

"Toasted, please," he replied, and she dropped the bagel halves into the matte finished, four-slot toaster. They worked together as if they had been together for years. Almost at the same instant they exchanged a look, which confirmed that they knew what the other was thinking.

Rick just *knew* they were on the same page.

Brandi knew they were not.

After they finished, Rick leaned back and lit his post-breakfast cigarette, his offer to help with the dishes being firmly denied. As Brandi peeked over her shoulder she noticed Rick's expression, which she interpreted as one of total contentment.

"Having fun yet?" Brandi asked with an air of sarcasm.

"Not at all," Rick replied in an inflection that couldn't have been further from the truth.

With the table cleared, it was again set with the same items that had occupied it the day before. The only new addition was a bottle of champagne to celebrate the completion of their labors.

Rick poured what was left of the brandy and vodka, draining each bottle.

After the bottles were trashed, Brandi began. "How does this sound? Lee arrives home from his trip, Wednesday or Friday, I'll find out when. His car is parked at the airport, so he'll be alone. He comes to the front door, noticing that it has been pried open. He yells out but hears nothing. He drops his luggage in the foyer and immediately heads into the house, heading for the closest phone in the living room. You'll be standing at the wall behind the light switch with a gun, knife, or the crowbar. You kill him. No alarm has been installed, and the house is far enough from the closest neighbor so no noise will reach them.

"When you first arrive, open some drawers, turn over some furniture. Make it look like a break-in. I'll be out with some friends, some public place where I will have an alibi. What do you think?"

Rick pondered the scenario. "Needs some work. I'll get a gun, an untraceable one. I don't want to leave any trace evidence behind, such as shoeprints in blood or fingerprints on any objects. We'll have to clean this place up good over the next several days. Forensics has come such a long way, they frighten me a bit. We'll begin by erasing any evidence of my visit. Toss out the bed sheets; pour drain cleaner down the faucets, vacuum the place, clean with bleach. After the deed is done, we can't have any contact for several weeks. I'll get a disposable cell phone— make that two—and we'll communicate in that manner."

"Geez, Rick, sounds like you've done this many times before," she said in a half-serious way.

"Who's to say I haven't?" he replied, trying to hold a serious look. "I just watch too much CSI, 48 Hours, and the like."

They embraced, squeezing each other simultaneously. They were newly formed partners in crime.

Rick reached for the bottle of champagne, but Brandi beat him to it. She twisted the wire netting clockwise, exposing the unobstructed cork. She firmly twisted the stopper, releasing a muffled "pop" as a misty spray curled and vanished into the air. She filled the glasses to an even level, nodding for him to raise it toward hers.

"To the continuation of the story of us," Brandi extolled.

All that remained was the *when*.

Chapter XXXVIII

That Sunday was an actual day off for Davis. He cleared it with the brass so that he would not have to be on call. He would not have to be accountable to anyone, barring a national disaster or alien invasion. He planned to visit his brother, Michael, and go to their favorite tavern for an afternoon of beer and baseball. One Sunday a month was reserved for the two siblings to have a real outing, a time when they didn't have to talk about work, obligations, or anything with a serious nature. They could let loose, act foolish, and carry on as they had done in less complicated times. Neither of them was involved in a serious relationship at the current time. Hence no need to ask permission from their girlfriends or spouses, a ritual that all of their married friends were required to perform.

Kelley and Caitlin were also enjoying the freedom of a Sunday for a newly married couple. They got a late start, continuing their late-night roll in the hay with a strong morning session. If the Russian Olympic judges had been given a bedside podium view, they may have scored unanimous 10s.

After lunch, the couple proceeded down the interstate toward Delaware Downs, a multifaceted entertainment complex complete with race track, casino, dining, and a hotel. Most of the wedding proceeds were stashed away for a starter home, so they grabbed a few hundred to try their luck at the tables. They started at blackjack and through the first hour broke about even. After several cocktails they moved over to the video poker machines, depositing forty dollars in neighboring bandits. Within the first five minutes, Caitlin hit five 7s, producing bells and flashing lights. A neatly groomed host in a suit and tie sauntered over, extending his hand toward Caitlin in a congratulatory manner. He reached into his pocket, and slipped a key into a side entry slot, disengaging the bells and whistles. Next he handed her an envelope with ten crisp new hundred dollar bills and wished them good luck. She slipped the envelope into her handbag, and they embraced their shared success and new fortune.

Gerald Eckland had taken the train down to Washington DC the previous evening, visiting a buddy from the FBI. It was both a social call and a business one, wanting to present the current case and investigation of Carl Mickels.

Ashley Stone was traveling down to Atlantic City with several of her girlfriends. Twice annually they would shop at the outlets, seeking out late summer bargains as the season came to a close. The group approached the 109 store project, determined to shop until they dropped. It would take most of the day.

Ellen Sue began her Sunday morning as she always did, working out. The only difference on this particular day was that she had received three free sessions to more of an upscale gym than the one she was attending. *Free is free, and change is good,* she thought, pressing a steel square at the entranceway. The two smoked glass doors opened inward to a small vestibule, and then the two see-through doors ahead followed suit. She entered into the health club lobby, which closer resembled a Fortune 500 reception area.

She was met at the desk by an attractive, physically sculptured blonde-haired woman in her mid-twenties. Ellen handed the day pass to "Traci," whose name badge was boldly displayed over her left breast.

"Welcome to New Attitudes, Ms. Diamond," Tracy said, glancing down at the name on the pass. "If you'd like, you can change and I'll give you the tour of our facilities."

"Let's take the tour first," she countered, already wearing her Nikes. All she needed was to grab a locker for her incidentals.

They proceeded around the oval-shaped reception area toward the left, following a sign marked **Training and Workout Arena**. It sounded more like a Hollywood set for *American Gladiators* than a good old American gymnasium. Traci started to explain all the amenities the club offered, such as separate pools for cardio training and laps. They also had a basketball court (which doubled as a volleyball court), the standard steam rooms and saunas, massage therapy three days a week, and sessions with the "Trainers for the Stars," offered at a small nominal fee.

Ellen Sue interrupted, asking what appeared to be a curious question. "Traci, are you from Northern Liberties or the Great Northeast?" Ellen Sue was a native Philadelphian and prided herself on her ability to detect the slightly different dialects of her hometown. Although Traci looked LA, she sounded Philly.

"Northern Liberties," came Traci's immediate response. She jokingly added, "You're pretty observant, yo."

They both girlishly giggled, the tour and canned speech being a little too salesperson-like for Ellen Sue's comfort level.

They continued the tour, walking and talking along the periphery of the one-sixteenth of a mile jogging oval. A female runner approached, her head looking down.

"How ya doing, Ms. Rand?" Traci chirped.

As she glanced up, Ellen Sue's eyes met with the woman's. It was Abbey Road, still being a person of interest (or at least bogus alibi) in regard to the open Carl Mickels case.

Ellen Sue glanced quickly at Traci and then back at the approaching woman.

"I know this woman too," Ellen Sue said, her voice's volume elevating as if in an interrogation room. "I know her as Abbey, Abbey Road, and she is currently involved in one unsolved Philadelphia homicide." Her loud volume was now causing the large workout room's metallic clanking of weights to dim. It also made the thirty-odd individuals working out to stop in their tracks and hone in on the center-stage show.

Traci's mouth was agape as Ellen Sue continued. "We'll be watching you, and we told you when you were down at the station to not leave town without checking in with us."

Abbey dropped her timid gaze, speeding up her pace and heading for the **women's locker room.**

Ellen Sue turned to Traci and apologized for the sudden outburst. She thanked her for the tour, mentioning that the fitness center was a little too far from her house but may see her again with her two remaining free passes.

As she headed for the exit, she smiled to herself, hoping she had stirred a sleeping dog.

By eleven o' clock that Sunday evening, each of the respective team members were in their respective beds. Without knowing, they all would have interesting stories to share in the break room the following morning.

Chapter XXXIX

Rick Grosse glanced at the time on the bottom right corner of his desktop. He reached for the highball glass resting on a souvenir coaster that depicted a large palm tree dwarfing the island of St. Maarten. He would take Brandi there after his upcoming project. The first murder had been done for survival, the second out of obligation and greed. The third, and undoubtedly final one, would be done for totally selfish reasons. He would recapture the woman who had gotten away, and this time he would do everything in his power to see that it would never happen again. It was this objective that was his sole motivation.

Noticing the ice cooling down his drink had melted, he rose and grabbed several new cubes. He picked up the half-empty fifth and replenished the level to his satisfaction. He now sipped the cool liquid and began to scribble some thoughts onto the yellow lined tablet.

Before he could jot down a single letter, his disposable phone rang. He identified the number of a similar phone he had given to Brandi. His caution and paranoia of any type of electronic trails was still noticeably in motion. Brandi too was impressed with his thoroughness, a trait absent from his adolescent years.

"Ricky, dearest, I miss you already," Brandi began. "I keep trying to tell myself this will work, it has to work. I'm so obsessing on the fact that I so, *so* much need it to work."

Rick, detecting the need for reassurance, responded in a confident manner. "I'm sitting here going over and over our plan. I called one of my old business associates, and he's getting me an untraceable gun, as well as a silencer. We don't want to wake the neighbors." Rick's attempt at some black humor failed to yield an immediate response, so he went on. "You must make sure that your alibi is ironclad. Make sure you're spending time on Wednesday with someone you know and trust—"

Before he could continue, Brandi interrupted. "Rick, I thought, didn't I say he's coming back tomorrow? His flight gets into Philly at 8:27." The tail end of the sentence was seemingly filled with an elevating level of concern on Brandi's part.

"I thought it was Wednesday! Wait ... tomorrow is fine. But we must go over the plan again. I want no chance of anything getting out of our control. If we control the situation and the playing field, we win the game." His statement projected an air of certainty. Without being face to face with her, he knew that he had just renewed her waning skepticism.

"I need to make some calls and final arrangements for tomorrow. Sit tight and don't worry about anything. I love you so much, and your knight in shining armor is mounting his steed." He knew it was kind of corny, but he didn't know how well Brandi performs under pressure.

Her voice snapped him out of his momentary tangent. "Mounting a steed sounds kind of kinky." Her response amused even herself as she laughed out loud, reassuring herself that she was in competent hands.

"Nice comeback. Very quick and funny," he said, noticing he had erased some of her nervousness. "I'll call early tomorrow morning, seven-ish, so we can figure out where to meet."

"Okay, Ricky. I feel a lot better now. Has anyone ever told you that you can make a person feel at ease, very easily? And have quite a sexy voice too, if I may say so."

He felt that tingle one gets when you are given a sincere and meaningful compliment from a person you deeply care about. Rick realized that they had only been reconnected for a minimal amount of time, but his sights were set on his perceived notion that they would spend eternity together.

Rick sipped another volume of the brandy, feeling a slight burn coat his throat, along with the usual head rush. He opened his small plastic bag of white powder and consumed an inch and a half worth in a steady stream. His head rush was rekindled, and a small surge of energy began to stimulate his mind. As he exhaled, a ring tone emanated from Abbey's designated phone.

"Rick, I ran into that bitch of a cop at the gym today!" The speed of her dialogue was nearing Mach 1.

"Slow down, Abbey," he said in the same reassuring tone he had just used during his conversation with Brandi. "What happened, where are you now?" he replied, noticing his speed was not far behind hers.

"It was this morning, and I'm just getting home now. She came into the gym and confronted me about the case, saying they would prove I was lying, and they won't give up until it's solved, and that they know—"

"Whoa, chill, slow down. They don't know jack, and they don't have shit. It's been almost four months, and if they had anything, we would be dragged down for questioning on a weekly basis. She's playing you, trying to get under your skin. Stay cool and it will all blow over in no time."

Rick's words made sense, but almost anything would if he had been drinking for a good part of the day and night. Rick heard what sounded like a brief sigh of relief, followed by an admission of overreacting. *Brandi was right*, he thought. He did have a way of settling one's nerves and lessening stress levels.

After Rick had offered to pay for a quick get-out-of-town vacation, she relented, apologizing for her panic attack. He told her to keep in touch and they would get together during the week to hang out. She thanked him and wished him goodnight as the connection vanished.

Rick repeated the process of his party ritual and picked up the pen as if it would help him regain his thought process. For the next half hour he projected the scene as if directing a crime show. The success of his plan hinged upon several factors. Her husband would have to arrive on or near schedule. Rick would have to enter the residence, unseen, walking the last several blocks as if invisible. Lee would have to die.

Tomorrow was going to be game day. Rick would begin his abstinence from any substance that would diminish his ability to accomplish his goal. He finished his cigarette, turned off the desk lamp, and headed toward the bedroom. Falling asleep would not come quickly, his heart and mind racing with tomorrow's main event.

CHAPTER XL

This particular Monday morning in August the sun making its predictable rise from the east as if a skilled puppeteer was gently tugging at its strings in a well timed motion. Davis heard the radio erupt, set to the local news, weather, and sports station. It was supposed to be a beautiful day, the forecasters calling for the mid-eighties, with an atypical low level of humidity. He reset the snooze button, wanting to organize the upcoming day's agenda his mind. He lay back on his pillow, closed his eyes, and imagined where this renewed investigation would lead.

In another part of the city Rick Grosse woke to a similar laundry list of things to do. He would meet Brandi for breakfast in an out-of-the-way place.

He needed to call Gando in order to pick up tonight's weapon du jour. Then he would pick up a common-looking wardrobe, purchasing sneakers two sizes too large, just in case he left any footprints. He thought it would also be a nice touch to leave some discarded cigarette butts from the nearest ash tray at the scene, further throwing off any forensic hotshots. He laughed, realizing he was watching too much television. He also needed to stop at his travel agent and purchase a flight to Mexico, possibly solidifying an alibi. He planned to meet Brandi a week or so later, after she took care of the loose ends associated with her unwanted spouse's demise. His nerves were currently calm, treating this day like any other at the office. He shuddered to think that he was becoming used to his new occupation.

The snooze alarm snapped Davis from his deep concentration. He threw off his comforter and headed for the kitchen to prepare the coffee.

A short while later he slid into his car. He'd promised to pick Ashley up, her car being in for service. He drove the several blocks. Upon pulling up to her entrance, she was holding two cups of steaming coffee.

The mandatory pastries were waiting in the conference room. The room was populated with most of the team from the OCTF, as well as some detectives borrowed for the upcoming surveillance. The crowd mulled around the breakfast nook, exchanging stories from the weekend, as well as pleasantries.

Davis stepped to the front of the room, slipping his pinkies inside the edge of his mouth. A loud whistle pierced the room, signaling for the day's assignments to begin.

"Good morning, team, and those who have so gracefully volunteered to help us with our new project. We will call this one 'Operation Pressure'. We have decided to devote a renewed interest in Mr. Grosse and his involvement—or presumed involvement— in the death of his partner, Carl Mickels. The plan is to follow his activities for the next several days. We need to investigate who he is seeing, doing some background checks on him."

Davis paused, sipping from his quickly cooling coffee mug. He continued. "Mr. Earl Reese will be assisting us with the legal maneuvers. Earl is an assistant US attorney, specializing in RICO cases as well as investigative techniques and loopholes we may have overlooked. He's damn good at what he does."

He turned to Earl, giving him the floor. "Ladies and gents, your boss was too generous with his accolades. I'm new to this position, having only six years of fieldwork. One thing about me, though, is that I have a full grasp of the law and have learned from some of the best, including the current attorney general, Nelson Silver. I will be refiling some search warrants, reinvestigating Mr. Grosse's past offenses, and in essence trying to get a grand jury indictment. Davis has supplied me with the files, and I do see some opportunities for the good guys. Thank you all, and I look forward to being of any assistance I can."

Sporadic applause echoed in the room as Davis approached center stage. He passed out several pages containing assignments, protocols, and partnering teams. Rick would be followed 24/7 along with Abbey Road. As Davis was talking shop, two teams were already waiting at the two suspects' residences. Additional teams would be leaving at noon. They knew that Grosse was both cautious and paranoid. They did not want him to spot the tails until it was decided to make their presence felt.

"In conclusion, as you all know, this is important for me. The case has been dragging on too long, and I refuse to let it slip into the cold case files. You're the team to get it done. Let's do it, and be careful out there."

The high-pitched sound of the classroom type chairs produced a symphony of noise as the members of the team rose and began Operation Pressure. If Reese could get one of his warrants approved, Geek would have his tracking device online. There was no chance for any screw-ups.

CHAPTER XLI

Rick did his morning ritual—getting out of bed, laying out his clothes, and if necessary, the manly trilogy: shit, shower, and shave.

After toweling off, he slipped into his clothes. He donned a generic Philadelphia Phillies T-shirt and cap, a perfect choice for blending into the city's several million inhabitants.

He picked up the phone to call Brandi. She answered on the second ring.

"Good morning, love," she cooed, sounding much more in control.

"I wish you were here this morning," he countered. "Now that we have reunited, I'm like a love-struck teenager."

"Soon I will be there with you. Not just for one day but all the time." She sounded sincere, and as always, so sexy.

Rick grabbed his keys and phone. He exited the building and hopped into the Mazda. He smiled. He couldn't imagine that after tonight, he would be reunited with the woman of his dreams. She was his beloved soul mate.

Rick punched in a number on the cell. He had an appointment with Gando, step one in the day's list of to-dos. As he pulled away from the curb, a nondescript Nissan did the same.

———————————

"He's proceeding south down Broad Street," Kelley reported. His partner today was Gina Maples, on loan from the detective squad. She was perky, smart, and well endowed. Kelley was newly married.

"I was reading the file on this scumbag," Gina said. "And I get the distinct idea that Davis is taking this a little to heart. Strange for a veteran cop."

"Bingo," replied Kelley. "We all want this guy. He has lots of connections, and if we could roll him or make some deal, the city will be a better place." Kind of clichéd, but Kelley was kind of mundane at times. "I think Davis liked Mickels. And no one takes kindly to your key witness being crushed under ten tons of concrete. I think Davis sees something else too. I think he's trying to link this case and the—" he paused and swallowed—"the bombing."

Gina took this info in and said nothing, not wanting to scrape old wounds.

Another unmarked car with two officers dressed in T-shirts and caps stayed a couple of blocks behind Kelley. They would switch positions at various times. Hell, it worked sometimes in the movies.

Rick made some turns off Broad Street, prior to where all the stadiums were. He pulled up to an auto body shop. It was called Low Rider, and a tall, Latin male emerge from the building. They were parked several blocks away, so Kelley grabbed the high-powered binoculars, focusing on the duo. Gina picked up the two-way radio, reporting the name of the business to Geek.

Kelley watched as they seemed engaged in small talk. He noticed laughing, hand motions, and head nodding. The listening device they had brought along would be way too obvious.

Geek's fingers caressed the computer keyboard as if it were a baby grand piano. The screen gave him all of the business info, as well as the owner's background. The owner, Miguel Booday, had about a dozen priors ranging from auto theft, possession, and several illegal handgun offences. Simultaneously, Kelley noticed a brown bag transferred from Miguel to Grosse. It was accompanied by each of them turning heads, as if to see if they were being watched. Grosse pulled what looked like a roll of cash from his pocket and slipped it into Miguel's open fist. They shook hands. Grosse then slipped the bag into the front pocket of his pants and returned to his car.

Gina broadcasted the play-by-play to Geek, and Geek responded with Miguel's priors. Grosse had just purchased drugs or weapons.

"Keep the tail on him. Do not, I repeat, do not pull the suspect over," Geek stressed emphatically.

"That's a copy," Gina replied.

Rick drove several blocks up Broad and took a turn closer to city hall. He pulled into a small lot that was for customers of a travel agency and a pet hospital. Since no dog was accompanying their suspect, they watched him enter the travel agency. The pair called it in. The backup team was alerted. Geek, listening in, told the backups to enter the agency after Grosse left and find out where the ticket was taking him.

Several minutes later he emerged, carry the unmistakably airline ticket envelope. He slid it into his back pocket and returned to the car. Gina and Kelley both noticed that he wasn't displaying his usual cautionary habits. He didn't look around, probably because he was confident or focused on his mission.

As he pulled out, Gina and Kelley followed. Out of the rearview mirror the backup team was observed entering the store. The results would be relayed to everyone involved, noting that a trip to Philadelphia International Airport could be the next destination.

They remained several blocks behind, heading further north away from the airport. They reported their observations. He drove down toward Delaware Avenue and parked in front of a Target store. He left the car, the bulge of the paper bag now missing from his trousers. They reported in again.

Not long after later he emerged carrying the branded white plastic bag with the red bull's-eyes advertising his shopping spree. They again reported his movements. It was a tedious series of events, but they hoped it would lead to something bigger.

Grosse headed back to Center City. He turned up the familiar street to his residence, left the car, and approached the building's front entrance. He was home, which meant nothing to do or the possibility that the day was over.

Geek's voice crackled in on the radio. "I received your last update. A new car is on the way. Switch vehicles with the others. I want no chance of your being made. Wait until ten o clock, and we will send in new blood to relieve you."

During the next several hours, new pieces were being added to the puzzle. Earl had been granted a seventy-two hour warrant, enabling the team to activate the tracking GPS they had mounted on the car. They had also learned that the ticket he'd purchased was a flight to Mexico City, one way, with a yet-to-be-determined return date. Common sense was that it was a stopover, a waiting area, or a permanent stay. They hoped they would find out sooner than later. Extradition was no picnic in the southern neighbor country.

The team following Abbey Road did nothing. It was late afternoon, and she had yet to emerge from her apartment. They did notice some well-groomed visitors entering the building. It was funny how they stayed for roughly an hour. If she was so good, they probably would have stayed for two. But all of them left with a big smile on their faces.

It was now past six o' clock, and they were getting hungry. Kelley sent Gina down the block for some sodas and hoagies.

Davis checked in, not having much more to add in regard to the day's events. It was all quiet on the Philly front.

Chapter LVII

As it approached seven o'clock, Rick began to ready himself. He took his obligatory shot of brandy, wondering if he really should switch to bourbon, and a line of white powder to clear his mind. It was a true anomaly as his two prior acts would probably produce a clouded mind. He proceeded to open the bag from Target, dumping its contents on the bed. He tore the tags off the dark, straight–legged, and neatly pressed trousers. He then slipped on a black T-shirt with a small front pocket. Sitting on the edge of the bed, he put on a pair of black Reeboks that were two sizes too big. If he picked up a black guitar, Johnny Cash would be proud.

He had to admit, meeting Miguel instead of Gando had spooked him a little. It wasn't uncommon for the mob boss to assign jobs like illegal guns to his affiliates, but for some reason Rick felt like he was being distanced from Gando. He hadn't heard from Gando in a few weeks besides the brief phone order Rick had placed for the gun.

Rick shook the feeling off. It wasn't like he was a sick dog being kicked out of the dog park. All that mattered was what he was doing for Brandi.

Davis and Stone were now sitting two blocks east of Grosse's residence. Kelley and Gina would stay mobile, backing the boss up. At seven thirty Grosse emerged, the new moon further camouflaging his evening outfit. He slipped into the front seat, appeared to adjust the rearview mirror, and took off.

Davis waited, not wanting to be spotted. He now had the luxury of watching his GPS, indicating the street and distance of the car he was tailing.

Geek's voice crackled over the radio. "Update," he broadcasted. "Ellen Sue and her partner have just finished interrogating Miguel. He had several warrants. They were conveniently waved after he admitted selling a Glock 19 and suppresser to our friend, Mr. Grosse."

They all knew this information would enable them reasonable cause to pull him over at any time. After weighing the options, they decided to wait until it was absolutely necessary and that no civilians were in harm's way.

Grosse turned on to the Schuylkill Expressway, the main artery leading to the northern suburbs.

They kept the car within the speed limit, hanging in the right lane as they left the city limits and entered Montgomery County.

Rick signaled he was leaving the expressway and entering the Mainline neighborhoods.

At this point, Davis backed off. A new team driving a BMW sedan honed in on the GPS and picked up the tail. After ten minutes of twisting through upscale neighborhoods, Rick's car's brake lights indicated it had arrived at the destination. The BMW proceeded a half block past and entered a vacant driveway. They hoped no one was home.

Another tail stopped two blocks before the house and cut the lights, and Gibson raised the night-vision goggles. Focused intently, he noticed Grosse emerge with what appeared to be a two-foot metal bar. He radioed his observations. Several cars pulled into the neighborhood, dispersing black-clad SWAT members who blended into the darkened night.

Grosse walked, slightly hunched in hopes it might decrease his visibility, toward a large English Tudor. Gibson watched through the goggles as Grosse pushed the flat end of the object into the space between the door and the jamb. On the second attempt the door splintered and Grosse shouldered the door open.

The SWAT team was alerted, and they efficiently surrounded the premises.

The house had been darkened as planned. Grosse was to wait behind the wall in the living room. It was approaching nine o'clock according to his watch. He placed his hand into his pocket and felt for the Glock and the tight-fitting silencer. At that moment a soft light permeated the room. Rick quickly glanced to his right.

The team was now positioned at several windows, and SWAT hovered at each entry and exit.

"My dearest Ricky, the love of my life," a soft voice projected from the nearby couch.

"Brandi? What the …?" Rick's voice squeaked in total shock.

A large long-barreled Remington Model 1911 was poised in Brandi's outstretched hand.

"Empty your pockets, Ricky, and stand where you are. Just place the gun down on the carpet."

Astonishment filled Rick's whole being, and before he could speak he complied with her demand.

"Let me explain," she began.

As Rick opened his mouth to speak, she ordered him to shut up and just listen for a change.

"Thirty-odd years ago, we were in love. Actually, we were pretty damn good for each other. At least we thought we were. Next you got me pregnant, and for this we're both to blame." She lifted a glass of white wine from the table, her eyes remaining fixed upon him. She continued. "Upon learning about this, what did you do? Let's see. You did absolutely fucking nothing. You ignored both me and the situation. My parents whisked me off to somewhere safe; somewhere we were unknown and could start again. Not once, *not one fucking time* did you try to find me. My friends told me you just bragged about it. Big man, real cool you were. I suffered, I was *miserable*, and I didn't know what to do. So I had the child, or at least thought I would. Then she died." Brandi was now on a roll. She was releasing all of the anger, hatred, and hostility she had built up against the person she felt had ruined her life.

"Brandi?" Ashley mouthed to Davis.

He shrugged a response. His face was steely rough.

Davis and Ashley listened intently as her tirade was unleashed. At the same time they quietly entered the foyer, which was obstructed from the living room. Ashley spotted a second entranceway that also opened to the living room. She bent down and approached it, using the wall as cover.

At the same time the scorn in Brandi's voice was intensely escalating. She continued: "I pulled my life together, made something of myself, and at the same time learned not to depend on anyone but myself. Ricky, dearest, I'm not married. I may be brilliant and devious, but I'm not married. You've been set up. My plan was, and is, foolproof. After I shoot you, I'll call the police and tell them I've shot a burglar. They'll notice the door has been forced open and poor, helpless me being so frightened grabbed my weapon in self defense. It is registered and totally legal. I then shot you, fearing for my life, and the case will not even last in the newspaper for more than two days. I will be a hero, admired by the NRA and women's groups for my brave actions." She began to laugh, and added, "I might even do the talk show circuit!"

At that instant, Davis and Ashley appeared from their respective entrances.

"Lower your weapon! Drop it on the floor! Now!" Davis demanded.

"Lay off, lady! Drop the gun!" Ashley shouted.

Both Brandi and Grosse turned their heads in utter amazement. In that frozen timeframe Grosse felt saved, but Brandi was pissed. Her years of planning the sweet revenge she had craved was now being compromised. Without thought, she turned the weapon toward Rick and pulled the trigger as fast as her finger could retract.

Rick's body collapsed to the floor in a limp and lifeless fluidity. Both Davis and Ashley fired their weapons at Brandi, as if programmed to react and not to think. Brandi tumbled off the couch, her gun falling from her hand, the shot glass swept away by her forward momentum. The amber fluid leaked onto the carpet, mingling with the swelling red pools.

The SWAT team rushed in upon hearing the gunfire, weapons at the ready. After seeing Davis and Ashley safe, they lowered their guns and approached the victims.

"This one's dead," said the first responder.

"Same here," added the other.

Davis picked the cell phone out of his pocket and called Geek. "Send a bus. They're both gone. I hope you have all that on tape; my microphone was loud and clear."

He asked Geek to gather the team back at the Roundhouse, wanting to share the story, courtesy of the recording. The techie agreed and prepped the SUV for the trip back downtown. CSI would gather the evidence, confirm the series of events, and clean up the bloody mess.

Ashley lifted the shot glass with a forefinger and thumb wrapped in a rubber glove. She sniffed the liquid, curious to find telltale poisonous odors. She laughed a little to herself.

Davis looked at her. "What is it?"

She gingerly sat the glass back down and stood. "Brandy. A shot of brandy. A little narcissistic, don't you think?"

"Would you prefer a shot of Ashley?" he asked, placing a hand over his mike to prevent being overheard.

"I think you would," she whispered back.

Epilogue

The sun danced through the circular windows that adorned the top floor of the Roundhouse. It was a perfect August day—low humidity, temperatures in the mid-eighties. The *Daily News* sat atop Davis's desk, the bold print reading **Mainline Headline**. It was a typical byline for the sensational story that followed.

Davis gave the obligatory news conference, recounting the series of events that had comprised this extraordinary case. He covered the murder of Carl, who had been paralyzed and then crushed to death in a heartless act of revenge. He embellished the team's tenacity in following up all leads and tips that had been generated by the story. He even mentioned that a witness had confirmed Rick Grosse leaving the building prior to its implosion. (It seemed Joey, the guard at the site, had lost a bout with his conscience and had come forth to volunteer the information. It didn't hurt that no charges would be leveled against him as an accomplice.) Davis mentioned also that a possible connection existed between Grosse and the bombing that had almost taken Kelley's life. According to the now cooperative Abbey Roads, Rick had supplied all the Philly mob boys' charms, which had gotten them into trouble with the Russians of Brighton Beach in the first place. Since crime families typically solve their own issues, the Russians had paid the boys back in a big way. It was estimated Kelley had simply been in the wrong place at the wrong time, as the saying goes.

As for the poison found in Mickels's system, where it came from remained a mystery. With all the contacts Rick Grosse kept on payroll he could have attained it from any number of sources. But anyone with information regarding the case was asked to contact the police tip line immediately.

Accommodations were bestowed upon all team members for the steadfastness they'd exhibited in seeing the case through. A celebration would follow at the Capitol Grille, which is strangely where Rick might have celebrated, had his plan been successful. Oh well.

Desert was served at Davis's apartment, and it was a party of two. Ashley would remark the following day that she got a ten-point match through APHIS on the shot glass fingerprints. No one was quite sure why that mattered, except for Davis.

Upon having breakfast at his favorite diner, Julian Gando flipped through *USA Today*. He scanned the section detailing the news from around the nation. When he saw the word *Pennsylvania*, he scanned the lone paragraph. It carried the story about a double murder that had taken place on Philadelphia's Mainline. The names of the victims were recognizable. He closed the paper.

The waitress approached to take his order.

"Steak and eggs, medium rare on the steak, and over easy on the eggs," he said. "Rye toast, large orange juice, and a decaf."

"Thanks, hon," the waitress replied. "Celebratory mood with that grin?"

Julian had just come into a lot of money, so he certainly did grin. "You got that right, sugar."

CPSIA information can be obtained at www.ICGtesting.com
Printed in the USA
BVOW010715180113

310993BV00001B/1/P

9 781462 066810